CONCRETE JUNGLE

Sam Harris Adventure Series

Book 7

PJ SKINNER

ISBN 978-1-913224-09-7

Cover design by Self Publishing Lab

Dedicated to all those who have joined me for Sam's adventures and stayed on to the end. It's been a blast.

Thank you

Discover other titles in the Sam Harris Series

Fool's Gold (Book 1)

Hitler's Finger (Book 2)

The Star of Simbako (Book 3)

The Pink Elephants (Book 4)

The Bonita Protocol (Book 5)

Digging Deeper (Book 6)

Go to the PJ Skinner website for more info
www.pjskinner.com

Chapter I

The ATM hiccupped and spat out a printed balance that summed up her dire financial state. There was no way she could buy a suit for tomorrow's interview. The unfairness of her situation almost made her weep. Sam Harris had worked as an exploration geologist in remote sites under extreme conditions for fifteen years, but she still had nothing to show for it. *How many thirty-nine-year-olds were living with their parents?*

Thoughts of the interview increased her stress levels to their breaking point. She had no idea what questions they would ask her, having never worked in mining finance before. *Could she persuade someone to take a chance on her or would she look like an idiot?* She would before she opened her mouth if she didn't find something suitable to wear, and fast.

There must be something in her wardrobe. She had worked in the field for most of her career, but hadn't she been dragged along to every social occasion invented for her entire adult life in a series of ghastly dresses and skirts purchased by her mother, an anathema to someone who lived in khaki?

Sam went home and enlisted the help of her mother, Matilda Harris, to review her options. She paraded a series of these outfits in front of a woman who, even with her advanced skills in encouragement, couldn't pretend they were suitable for a city interview. Her anxiety mounted as each outfit failed the test.

'Let's ring Hannah,' her mother said. 'She'll have something you can wear.'

Sam sighed. Hannah, Sam's elder sister, at least a size smaller than her, held an attitude to Sam's clothes which only just fell on the sisterly side of scathing. But her mother ignored the sigh and picked up the receiver, dialling the number from memory.

'Hello, darling. We're in a spot of bother. Sam has an interview tomorrow, and she has nothing to wear. Can you help?'

She listened to the answer, frowned and nodded.

'Yes, I know it's late notice. What about tomorrow morning before work?'

Grumpy sounds issued from the receiver which indicated Hannah's displeasure with this idea.

'It can't be helped, sweetheart. It's an emergency,' said Matilda.

The next morning, a dishevelled Sam knocked on the door of her sister's flat before it got light. Squeals of delight prefaced the door opening by her nephew and his sister who launched themselves at her legs.

'Where's your mummy then?' said Sam.

Hannah appeared in the corridor, already immaculate, her wavy blonde hair in a chignon and her face made up to appear make-up free. Sam shrugged at her and gave her an impish grin.

'Sorry, sis, I couldn't dissuade our mother. She thinks you're the Trinny Woodall of the Harris family,' she said.

'It's not her fault you don't have any clothes. I should volunteer you for an episode in the next series.'

'I'd buy something myself if I wasn't broke.'

'If your industry didn't rise and fall like a rollercoaster, you'd have plenty of money. You chose the wrong career,' said Hannah.

'Too late now,' said Sam.

'Let's see,' her sister said, walking around Sam like a farmer examining a horse. 'It looks as if you are eating too much of Mummy's delicious cooking. I don't think I've got much that will fit you. Perhaps the suit I wore when I was pregnant.'

Sam brindled but didn't rise to the bait. She carried a few extra pounds gained during a year's sitting at a desk swotting for her one-year intensive Master's degree, but she had never been fat. Her sister had had two children but possessed a figure like a slim nineteen-year-old. Genetics.

Hannah produced the suit from her wardrobe. A plastic cover from the dry cleaners still covered it. Sam ripped it off and examined the suit. Its padded shoulders gave it a dated air but beggars could not be fashion models. She pulled off her jeans and T-shirt with reluctance and Hannah helped her into the suit.

'Honestly, Sam. You're not in the jungle now. Can't you keep still for one minute? It's like trying to dress a toddler.'

A rhetorical question to which Hannah knew the answer. She tugged at the hem of Sam's skirt and tutted. Sam grinned at their reflection in the mirror. The sisters were like chalk and cheese despite their physical similarity. Awkward in her power suit with its padded shoulders and pencil skirt, Sam glanced at her sister with something approaching envy.

Hannah wore an almost identical suit, but she radiated style and elegance with her blue eyes and blonde hair. Despite Hannah's best efforts, Sam didn't come close. Her light brown hair refused to stay in its bun, and the skirt strained at the seams where she forced the zip up. She held her stomach in and waited for Hannah's appraisal.

'Okay. That's the best I can do. You look professional,' said Hannah, standing back and admiring her work.

'Thank you. I'll buy my own suit once I get my first salary. The master's degree cleaned me out.'

'Money well spent. It's the start of your new life. I'm proud of you.'

Sam beamed. Her relationship with Hannah revived after her brush with death in Tamazia, helped because Hannah divorced Sam's ex-boyfriend and he had vanished without a trace. Without Simon between them, life became a lot less complicated.

'Good luck today, sis.'

'Thanks. I'll need it.'

Sam checked her shoulders for rebel hairs straying from her bun of ruler-straight hair. Her green eyes glistened at the thought of the challenges ahead.

'Oh my God! Have you seen the time? I've still got to take the children to school. I'll be late for work,' said Hannah.

'What about my interview?' said Sam. 'I've should leave right now. Thank you for the suit, and the shoes.'

Sam rushed to the tube station, fighting the tight skirt, her heart pounding. She forced her way into a crowded carriage and travelled the few stops to Green Park with someone's briefcase sticking into her back. She travelled up the escalator and tottered out into the street, turning to read the street signs to locate herself. The heel of her shoe slipped into a grating and twisted off leaving her prone on the pavement with the contents of her handbag being kicked up the road by the rush-hour crowd emerging from the station.

Flushed with embarrassment she righted herself and crouched down to pick up her notebook, tissues and the other habitual residents of her bag. A man walked straight into her and knocked her back onto the ground. He didn't break stride. Sam staggered to her feet and noticed that her knee had a graze and a massive ladder now ran all the way down her leg.

She looked at her watch and almost fainted. *Five minutes? Which was worse, arriving on time without a heel on her shoe, or arriving late with her heel attached?* She chose the latter, buying a tube of superglue and sticking the heel back on. Then she waited a few minutes for it to cure, trying not to glance at her watch again.

This whole job interview scenario was a lot more stressful than she had expected. After a narrow escape from her last job in Tamazia had persuaded her to try working in a city, Sam used her savings to do a master's degree in business administration. The intensive one-year MBA course tested her resolve, but ten years of seven-day weeks in the field had prepared her for the workload, and she coasted through without excelling.

Getting a job in London proved to be a lot harder than the master's degree. Her resume sat neglected on recruiters' desks, despite her effort to emphasis her skill set and Master's degree. Despite her new qualification and wide international experience, they did not offer her any interviews. Transferable skills meant nothing when her resume contained only geology jobs in countries most recruitment agents had never heard of. Nobody seemed interested in her problem-solving skills or her ability to speak several languages.

'You're a square peg in a round hole.'

'Don't you think you're a little old to start a new career?'

She became desperate for work and should have been thrilled to get an interview, but an analyst position with a tiny mining broker she had never heard of did not appeal to her. A recruitment agency based in the City of London set it up for her. The recruiter who called her sounded as if he was fifteen years old and didn't know the difference between a geologist and an engineer. Not an encouraging start.

'It's perfect for you. They're desperate for someone with your experience,' he said.

They appeared desperate. *What sort of company offered such an eye-watering salary to a person with no financial experience?* Not that Sam was a stranger to Excel, but, in the past, numbers had been something she fobbed off on someone else. Getting the MBA convinced her it was only in the mind. This was her chance to forge a new career, and she intended to take it.

She shoved her shoe back on, struggling to balance in her tight skirt, and hobbled down the street, trying not to put too much weight on the newly glued heel. Dover Street was a short walk from Green Park underground station, but blisters had erupted on her feet by the time she arrived at the Georgian three-story house with a loft extension sticking above the two houses on either side of it. Hannah's shoes were half a size too small for her and she hadn't worn heels since her cousin's wedding the year before. Another purchase to make with her first salary.

The newly-painted blue door did not yield to her cautious push. Three rusty screws attached an entry phone with four grimy buzzers to the door frame. The labels were almost illegible and one had peeled off. A new sticker on the top buzzer read Resource Ventures Inc. She took two deep breaths, letting them out with exaggerated slowness to still her racing heartbeat. Then she rang the doorbell.

A lilting Scottish accent with London overtones issued from the speaker making Sam jump.

'Hello, is that Sam?'

'Um, yes, it's me. I'm sorry I'm a little late.'

'That's okay. Leo's still on a call. Push the door hard and come up the stairs. We're on the top floor.'

The stairs to the loft office were narrow, steep, bare boards with splashes of white paint. As she negotiated them in her tight skirt, Sam's anticipation turned to disappointment. She had expected chrome and glass, and silent elevators. *What sort of company was this?* As she reached out to knock on the door, she felt the zip on her skirt give way. Too late to do anything now. She pulled her jacket down over the skirt and waited for the door to open.

Chapter II

Edward Beckett could pinpoint the exact moment his world fell apart for good. On an otherwise perfect Sunday afternoon, a knock at the door of his house in central London sent his comfortable life into a downward spiral.

He had lunched on roast lamb with mint sauce at the local pub with his wife Ophelia, and afterwards, they relaxed in the sitting room, steaming cups of coffee by their sides. Parts of the *Sunday Times* and the *Sunday Express* lay scattered around the sofas and coffee table. Someone rang the doorbell, causing him immense irritation, and Ophelia went to answer it, as the housekeeper had the day off.

'Who is it?' he said.

If Ophelia answered, he hadn't heard her. He stood up, intending to aid her in sending away the Mormons, or whoever had disturbed their afternoon reading the Sunday newspapers. Ophelia came back into the room, her Botox-ravaged faced devoid of expression. Shock had drained the blood from her cheeks. She seemed unable to speak. Edward wrinkled his brow.

'What on earth's wrong? Has someone died?'

She gazed at him as if she had found an alien in the sitting room. The side of her lip rose in a snarl.

'No, but you'll soon wish you had.'

Before he could react, she moved aside to reveal the smug, plump face of Steven Horgan. Edward opened his mouth, but it was his turn to be speechless.

'Hi, Dad,' said Steven.

The memory infuriated him. Edward slammed his fist onto the countertop, splashing coffee onto the faux marble surface. He ripped several pieces of paper towel from the roller fixed under the kitchen cabinets, taking a lump of skin from his knuckle on the metal runner at the bottom of the door.

This brought him to tears of self-pity. A drop of blood fell into the puddle of coffee and spread into it like a tie-dye. He mopped it up, screwed the paper towel into a ball and threw it at the rubbish bin. It bounced off and rolled on the floor.

He sat on an uncomfortable stool with a short metal back and sipped the hot liquid, grinding his teeth with fury. Since the untimely appearance of his son, a bewildering tornado of bad luck and coincidence had reduced his life to this. Gone was his magnificent Georgian terraced house in Regents Park, replaced by this dump which looked like no one redecorated it since the nineteen-seventies. With it went his wife and their elegant lifestyle.

Like many people born with a silver spoon in their mouths, Edward Beckett was ill-suited to cope with adversity. Since birth, his life had revolved around the social calendar; Cheltenham, the Grand National, the Boat Race, Badminton Horse Trials, Glyndebourne, Ascot, Wimbledon and Henley every year. The nearest he got to jeopardy was shooting grouse on the estates of his friends after the glorious twelfth.

He had married a suitable girl from amongst the ranks of the last debutantes presented to the queen and settled down to a privileged life in a house in Regent's Park with nothing more taxing than the occasional visit to the stockbrokers to talk about the value of his inherited fortune.

The first sign that things were not going as planned was the absence of an heir. Try as they might, they remained childless, and he endured suggestions he was *shooting blanks*. This induced a longing to prove himself in other ways and he launched his own investment fund. His ability to spot a winner in a rising market soon led to a reputation for high performance. His clients and colleagues lionised him and he gained a reputation for ferocity that terrified many of them.

The stock market crash of 1987, which decimated his portfolio, shook the foundations of his charmed existence. He claimed to have recovered it all in the months that followed but his aura of invincibility faded. Panic set in as he put his money in ever more outlandish schemes trying to recuperate his losses. He transferred money back and forth between funds to cover it up.

To make matters worse, he was being blackmailed. A liaison with Amanda Horgan, a young woman from Sydenham, produced his longed-for son, but she wanted him to divorce Ophelia and he had no intention of leaving his wife for someone of a lower social class. It was not as if he got her pregnant on purpose. In the early days of their relationship, she was all over him like a rash. He didn't feel guilty. His friends were all at it like rabbits with anyone who wanted a touch of the high life.

But when he refused to marry her, Amanda went nuclear. She threatened to expose him to his barren wife, and he resorted to begging and pleading followed by bribery. After extended negotiations, he bought her a little house in Beckenham and deposited a monthly stipend into her account. This produced the required effect and their relationship lasted despite his reluctance to do the decent thing. He found he couldn't resist visiting Amanda once a month and checking on the progress of his son, Steven. The little boy soon learned how to manipulate his absent father and made sure he squeezed every penny he could out of Edward.

When the boy needed a good secondary school, Edward put the boat out. He pulled every string he could to get Steven into Eton where he did not shine because of his lazy and entitled nature. He managed respectable grades with the help of a private tutor after Edward realised that Steven might emerge with no qualifications.

During the good years, Edward could hide these expenses from Ophelia but recently it became impossible. Added to that, Steven threatened to turn up at Edward's house demanding money and recognition as his son. By sheer luck, Ophelia didn't come across any evidence of Steven's existence, but it was only a matter of time as Edward fought to keep them apart. And then Mike Morton put his size elevens right in it.

Mike Morton had a lot to answer for. The man possessed all the subtlety of a bison on heat. He was a typical product of a rough upbringing in the East End; desperate to escape his clichéd childhood and willing to do almost anything to achieve it. Despite being from such different backgrounds they had a lot in common, a love of money being their principal driver. Mike had plenty of great ideas and Edward owned the money to make them a reality.

In the beginning, Edward enjoyed having a cockney friend, so different from his Eton schoolmates, but over the years the novelty wore thin as Mike borrowed increasing amounts of money from him for his outlandish schemes. The worst transgression had been an investment in Sierramar. They put money into the budding exploration market in the country and ended up on a hunt for Inca Treasure. They hired a female geologist, Sam something, and she stumbled across a set of Inca steps in the jungle. The hunt ended in a fiasco when the Indians guarding the treasure had sneaked off with it leaving them empty-handed, or at least that's the story Mike fed him. He had never trusted Mike since then.

When Mike made a fortune in the dot-com boom, Edward's annoyance turned to jealousy and dislike. And giving Edward's address to Steven? What a massive mistake. That was the final insult. Edward told Mike that Ophelia knew all about his progeny with Amanda Horgan, and introduced him to Mike as his heir, but that wasn't an excuse for his stupid action.

He could see no escape from his predicament. At least he hid his ownership of the office from Ophelia's lawyers. They had taken almost everything else. His partnership with Leo Giustra, the broker, represented his last chance of making money and he turned out to be worse than useless, not helped by Steven who had blackmailed Edward into getting him a job with Leo.

Even his gentleman's club blackballed him after he failed to pay his annual subscription. Soon, the news of his reduced circumstances would spread, and his circle would ostracise him. He had to get back on track or he would be finished.

Chapter III

The October sunshine had heated the attic boardroom to a stifling temperature. Kelly Maguire opened the skylights and placed a fan in the corner to blow the muggy air out. She moved a vase of blue iris flowers from the meeting table and sprayed it with polish. Then she rubbed it until it shone, her arm flexing in her tight shift dress with diamante bordering at the collar.

She reached across the top, teetering on her skyscraper stilettos. Her auburn hair fell out of its bun over her face. It matched the colour of the table except for a blonde streak in the front. A low whistle broke her concentration. Her pretty face with its big blue eyes screwed up in a grimace hidden from the source of the catcall.

'I've got to get me some of that,' said Steven Horgan, who was leering at her backside.

She spun around with the can of polish in her hand, pointing the nozzle at his face in defiance, knowing while Leo Giustra wanted her around, Steven could not touch her.

'It's two pounds and fifty pence in the supermarket,' she said. 'What do you want?'

'Nothing. Just going out to a meeting. I'll be back after lunch.'

She let out the breath she had been holding. Live to fight another day.

'Okay. Have a good one.'

Her boss, Leo, had asked her to time his interview with Sam Harris, the candidate for the analyst position, to coincide with Horgan's habit of slipping out for long lunches on a Friday.

'I don't want him interfering. She's new to the City and may not be ready for his brand of enthusiasm.'

Kelly pursed her lips.

'Sam's a woman? I assumed you were interviewing a man. Isn't it unusual to find a female mining analyst?' she said.

'They're like hen's teeth, but she's got an MBA, and she speaks French and Spanish. Added to that, she has ten years' experience working in the field, something Steven has never done. I'm convinced she'll be our secret weapon. I'll send you her resume so you can have a peep.'

Kelly read Sam's resume with growing respect. Sierramar, Simbako, Lumbono, and Tamazia. Tamazia! Something floated in her memory, just out of reach. A kidnapping or hostages? She pictured a stout middle-aged woman in tweed, with a bit of moustache and laddered tights. Not Horgan's cup of tea at all.

Maybe Leo was right. If this woman had been successful in these remote environments, perhaps the City would not be as challenging for her as it was for most women trying to break into the lads-only culture left over from the 1980s. *Whatever happens, she won't be alone while I'm around.*

***

The door at the top of the stairs opened and a petite woman with smiling eyes stood in the doorway.

'I'm Kelly Maguire, Leo Giustra's personal assistant. Sorry about the stairs. We haven't got around to carpeting them yet.'

'Nice to meet you,' said Sam, hovering on the top stair, uncertain if she should comment.

'Come in. Leo's busy right now but I printed out a summary of our projects for you to read so you can familiarise yourself with what we do here. Do you want something to drink? There's water on the sideboard or I can get you a tea or a coffee?'

'Water will be fine, thank you.'

Kelly showed Sam into the meeting room with its skylights and polished table. A whiteboard, with coloured marker pens in its tray, sat in one corner. Sam's spirits lifted as she sipped a cool glass of water and collected her thoughts. *I didn't apply for this job; they asked for me.* She picked up the report and flicked through the contents.

Since being involved in a stock market manipulation attempted by Bonita Mining several years earlier, Sam had developed a keen interest in the workings of the market for mining shares, focussing on junior companies involved in exploration. This passion had increased as she progressed through her MBA, and she had written her dissertation on the junior mining markets. The document in front of her contained prime examples of the pitfalls awaiting the unwary investor and an unusual sensation of smugness settled over her. *I've got this.*

The door burst open and Leo Giustra bustled in, beaming. Beads of sweat sat on his forehead and he mopped it with a massive handkerchief which he stuck into the pocket of his well-worn suit. Sam stood up and shook his damp hand, resisting the temptation to dry her hand on her skirt. She pulled her jacket down over the broken zip, relieved that she had her back to the wall.

'Sit, sit,' her host said. 'Has Kelly offered you a coffee?'

'Yes, thank you.'

Sam sat down again. Leo seemed unsure where to start. Then he noticed the document on the table in front of Sam.

'Ah, you've seen our portfolio. What do you think?'

Sam bit her lip, struggling to find something polite to say. *Come on, now or never.* Leo, who had watched her reaction, sighed.

'Do you know why you're here?' he said.

'Not really,' said Sam, relieved at not having to comment on the portfolio.

'Our investments have all been disasters,' he said, shrugging. 'I used to invest in major companies with a top-six broker firm in Canada. We worked off spreadsheets and production forecasts. I went out on my own during the last mining boom in Toronto and I got slaughtered in the aftermath of the Granoro scam. My partner bailed me out. We left Toronto and set up in London.'

Sam was dying to interject with her experience of the Bonita Mining debacle, but now was not the time to be indiscreet about former employers.

'That whole thing was a train wreck,' she said. 'Lots of people got their fingers burned.'

'Like me. Anyway, we started this small operation about a year ago and so far, we have picked only duds.

We need someone to sort the wheat from the chaff in the junior sector, and when I asked the agency for the best candidate, they sent us your resume.'

Sam felt the colour rise in her cheeks.

'Who's your partner?' she said.

'He prefers to remain anonymous due to a conflict of interests. Mostly he lets me get on with it.' He winked. 'Let's get down to the nitty-gritty, shall we? I'd like to know your philosophy on picking a winner in the junior market, since I understand that you wrote about it for your dissertation.'

'Can I use the whiteboard?' said Sam.

'Sure, knock yourself out.'

As soon as she started to write, all her nerves disappeared, and the broken zip faded from her mind. She had Leo's total attention.

'Only one greenfields exploration project in a thousand becomes a mine,' said Sam, drawing a triangle on the board. 'So there are a lot of duds out there. At each stage in exploration, some projects fall by the wayside.' She inserted numbers at each level in the triangle. 'The biggest mistake is to calculate their worth using numbers alone.'

'What do you suggest?'

'I use three criteria to judge a project. Is there any mineral or metal there, can they get it out, and who will do it?'

'The mineral thing is obvious, right? No gold, no mine. But what about the other two?' said Leo.

'The "can they get it out" question encompasses the technical, legal, political and environmental side of the project and depends on where the project is located. How friendly is the mining law, is the tax burden too heavy, can you export the product for dollar income? That sort of thing.'

'And the who?'

'Success breeds success. I prefer a team with a track record in junior companies. Who's done this before and have they sold out to a major at any stage.'

'That makes sense, but does it work?'

Sam laughed.

'Theoretically, yes. I used these criteria to grade junior companies in my dissertation and they were a good indicator of success.'

'Who have you worked for in the City?'

Sam's face fell despite herself.

'Oh, I haven't worked in London yet. I ran exploration projects in South America and Africa prior to starting the MBA.'

'You haven't done this before?' said Leo.

Sam registered the disappointment in his voice. Refusing to let it thwart her, she countered.

'No, but I have a lot of experience working in junior companies so I have insider knowledge few office-based analysts have. That's not something you can learn secondhand.'

Leo sat back in his chair and rubbed his sideburns. Sam waited, resisting the temptation to fiddle with her pen, her confidence evaporating. Leo leaned forward again.

'Would you read one of our projects over the weekend and give me an opinion on it?'

'Like a test?'

'It would give me an idea of your fit for this job ahead of my final decision.'

Sam never looked a gift horse in the mouth.

'That would interest both of us. I'll email you my summary on Monday.'

'Email it to Kelly, please. I'm not great at new technology yet. I might delete it by mistake.'

Kelly Maguire appeared at the door.

'Leo, I'm sorry to disturb you, but your conference call starts in five minutes.'

'Drat, I forgot. Can you print out our non-disclosure agreement for Sam to sign, please? And a copy of the Fair Isle project report. Okay, Sam, it was great to meet you. We'll be in touch.'

Sam floated back to her parent's house, blisters and zip forgotten. She boiled the kettle and poured the water onto a teabag in her favourite mug, humming along with the radio. The telephone rang before she had fished out the teabag. The recruitment agent's voice, an octave higher with excitement, echoed in her ear.

'How did the interview go? I expect you made quite an impression on Leo.'

'Pretty well. He wants me to review a project ahead of his decision. To see what I know, I imagine.'

'That's most irregular,' he said. 'I don't recommend it.'

'If it goes well, I'll start full time with them,' said Sam. 'It's the perfect solution.'

'What about my commission?' said the agent.

'It will have to wait,' said Sam.

***

Sam made sure Leo received her review of the project by going back to the office in Dorset Street and handing it to him in person. He turned the piece of paper over as if to check for more writing on the back

'Short and sweet uh?' he said.

Sam bit her lip.

'Um, well, once I spotted the fatal flaw...'

Leo raised an eyebrow.

'And what was that?' he said.

'The exploration concession had only six months to run and was non-renewable under the new mining law. The company hadn't got time to carry out the programme they committed to under their agreement with the mining institute. They would have lost the concession, and your investors their money.'

Leo guffawed.

'Ha! Where have you been all my life?' he said. 'Welcome to Resource Ventures. I'll talk to the recruitment agent today.'

He folded the summary, shoving it into his pocket.

'I'm rushing out now. I understand you're having lunch with Kelly today. Why don't you wait in the boardroom?'

He shook Sam's hand and left, disappearing down the stairs. Sam entered the boardroom where she found an old newspaper on a chair. She flipped through the sports pages, hoping to read a report on the autumn rugby internationals, oblivious to Steven Horgan who appeared in the doorway. He came up behind her and slammed his hand down on her shoulder to advertise his presence.

Sam yelped in pain and surprise and spun around in her chair to find his face shoved right up against hers. She could smell coffee and cigarettes on his breath.

'You think you're so clever,' he hissed. 'Don't get too cocky. You'll never work here if I've got anything to do with it.'

Before she could answer, he left. Sam rubbed her shoulder, shaken by his vehement reaction. *Who the hell was that, and what was his problem?* Her mood dropped from euphoric to depressed in an instant.

'Are you coming?'

Kelly Maguire appeared, balanced on a pair of heels so high they almost raised her toes off the floor, her blonde quiff brushed back onto her brown hair. She noticed Sam's face.

'You won't stand me up, will you?'

She wanted to, but it wasn't an option.

'No, I'm coming.'

She grabbed her bag and followed Kelly down the steep stairs into the street.

'Fish and chips in the pub?' said Kelly. 'It's Friday.'

'Sounds good,' said Sam, dredging up some enthusiasm.

The Coach and Horses teetered on the corner of Bruton Street, looking much as it would have on the day it opened in 1770. The women made their way up the rickety stairs into a snug upstairs bar with shiny, beer-stained, wooden tables. A smiling young woman took their order for fish and chips with two drinks.

'How did it go with Leo?' said Kelly.

'He offered me the job,' said Sam. 'But...'

She gazed at her food, trying to stop the lump rising in her throat.

'But what? Spit it out. I can keep a secret.'

Although she found this unlikely, Sam told the truth.

'A man who works in your office threatened me and told me not to take the job.'

Kelly's eyes opened wide.

'Who did? Describe him.'

'Young, plump, sandy-haired. It happened in seconds, then he disappeared.'

'Behind you? That sounds like Steven. He's a jerk. What was his problem?'

'I'm invading his territory. Given the lack of success he's had, I suppose he's feeling insecure. He doesn't want anyone policing his projects.'

'But you can't take him seriously. Leo won't let him disrespect you. Neither will I.'

Sam shook her head.

'I can't bear any more sexist Neanderthals telling me what to do. I'll find another position.'

'That little toad. Are you sure you want to turn this down? We can deal with Horgan together.'

'I just can't face it. I've spent years being treated like a second-class citizen. My tolerance has evaporated.'

'I'd like to tell Leo what happened.'

'Don't. I'm disappointed because I had set my heart on working with you and Leo. I can't cope with a large broker yet. But Horgan is a dealbreaker.'

Kelly flicked her hair back as if dismissing the subject, causing several patrons to cast admiring glances in her direction. She oozed sex appeal and confidence.

'How's your love life?' she said.

'Mine? Ha! None existent. The odd bonk in extremis, and that's about it,' said Sam.

'I'd have guessed they were swarming about you like bees around a queen.'

'I've been on the shelf for years. It's not so bad up here. The view's great.'

'I can't believe that. You're in no way past it.'

'I'm thirty-eight.'

'What? I estimated you were about twenty-eight. What moisturiser are you using? I must know.'

Sam laughed.

'I feel eighty-eight some days. How about you?'

'I'm on my second marriage. He's ex-Army and does press-ups in the bedroom.'

'I hope you're underneath. Never miss an opportunity.'

Chapter IV

When Leo had not heard from Sam or the recruitment agent for several days, he fretted. He picked up the telephone and buzzed through to Kelly.

'Put me through to the recruitment fellow, please, and get me a tuna sandwich. I'm staying in for lunch.'

A few moments later, she stood at the door to his office. 'He's on line one.'

Leo grabbed the receiver and poked the button flashing on the keyboard.

'Hello?'

'Hello, Mr Giustra, it's Fred Willis here. How can I help you?'

'It's about Sam Harris. I'm impatient to get her on board. Has she signed the contract yet?'

'I'm sorry. I thought my partner had called you. I'm afraid Miss Harris won't be joining you.'

'What? How did that happen? I offered her the job.'

'There's nothing I can do. She called us a few days ago and turned it down. It's unusual, but it happens occasionally.'

'But why? I thought we got on so well. She's perfect for the position.'

'She wouldn't say. I'm as disappointed as you are. I thought she was a great fit.'

'Maybe she got a better offer?' said Leo.

'It's possible. Anyway, water under the bridge now. Are you still looking for someone? We have several other candidates if you would like me to send their resumes?'

'Are they the same ones you sent me last month?'

'Yes. There are some great people in there.'

'Give me some time to re-read them and I'll get back to you if there is anyone I fancy meeting.'

'Don't leave it too long. Candidates like these get snapped up in an instant.'

So how come they were still available after a month?

'Okay, thanks.'

After the call, Leo ruminated in his office, his black mood not helped by the memory of Steven's smug face when he heard about Sam. Kelly brought him a cup of coffee and waited for the usual effusive praise and thanks. When none was forthcoming, she wrinkled her brow and examined his slumped shoulders.

'What's up, Leo? Can I help?' she said.

'It's Sam. She turned down the job. I can't understand it. I thought we had chemistry.'

He stuck out his bottom lip like a petulant child. Kelly hesitated.

'What?' he said.

'Nothing. It's just disappointing,' she said. 'I was looking forward to working with her.'

'So was I.'

Leo's day did not improve. One of their client companies tanked on the stock exchange after their drilling results got delayed, and their technical director resigned. It was only a matter of time before irate investors called the office. Leo called Steven into his office for a debrief.

'It's a nightmare. Shouldn't we have had prior knowledge of this?' said Leo Giustra.

By 'we', he meant 'you', and the inference would have been clear to anyone listening, but Steven Horgan, who had the skin of a rhinoceros and the survival skills of a cockroach, did not appear to notice.

'These things happen. The numbers don't lie,' said Steven, chewing vigorously on his habitual stick of gum, his cheek muscles flexing.

Leo put his head in his hands and sighed, a hoarse sound emanating from cigarette-clogged lungs. His bald head shone under the fluorescent lights, the remaining hairs forming fuzzy forests around his ears and over his collar line. He had luxuriant sideburns invaded with silver hairs which threatened a complete takeover. He blew out another breath over his thick lips and raised his round, protruding eyes to the man who had blocked out the natural light by standing under the skylight.

'They've lied this time. This project is a crock of shit.'

'I wouldn't say that.' Steven smirked.

'Oh? And what would you say? The share price has plummeted since we invested. What would you like me to tell the investors?'

Steven, who had sold his shares short at a tidy profit, shrugged.

'I don't know. Isn't that your job?'

Leo stood, his fists clenched at the end of plump arms held tight to his sides.

'This is your problem,' he hissed. 'You tell them. And get out now before I say something I regret.'

Horgan grinned at his impotence. 'Right oh,' he said, without the slightest intention of telling anyone. 'I'll do it after lunch.'

He left Leo's office flicking a balled-up blue wrapper from a piece of chewing gum into the waste-paper basket in the corner. The ball of paper hit the side of the basket and rolled onto the floor.

Leo Giustra flopped back into his seat. Having extricated himself from a tricky financial situation during the crash in mining shares caused by the Granoro scam on the Toronto Stock Exchange, he had accepted help from Edward Beckett, a London financier, to get set up in London. His small broker's office occupied the attic flat of a building belonging to the Beckett family trust, through a series of offshore companies, making its ownership hard to trace.

Taking on Steven had been one condition for using the office, one which Leo regretted agreeing to more every day. If Leo didn't make some money, he could never escape his position as the frontman and scapegoat for the Beckett money-making machine. *I'm not taking this anymore. If I could get my hands on a good analyst, I could make enough money to move and rid myself of the Becketts and their relatives.*

Kelly Maguire returned from the sandwich shop to Dorset Street to find Leo in his office with his head in his hands. He lifted it as she came in with his customary cup of coffee.

'Good afternoon,' she said. 'Are you all right? You look terrible.'

'I've been worse but not much. Another one of Steven's projects has turned out to be crap. I can't face ringing the investors.'

'Why do you put up with him?'

'His father owns the office and I can't afford to move out if we don't make some money. But if we keep Steven, we won't make any money. It's a vicious circle.'

Kelly lingered in the doorway.

'What's the solution?' she said.

'I thought Sam was, but then she turned down the job. I just don't get it.'

'What about the new candidates the agency sent you?'

'None of them come close. She had talent and guts, and we hit it off. I don't understand what happened.'

'Is Steven here yet?'

'Is that a joke? He's gone to lunch again. Who knows if he'll bother to turn up again today?'

'One second…'

Kelly went down the passageway to check Steven's office and then she came back into Leo's pushing the door shut with her foot and lowering her voice just in case.

'I know why Sam didn't come on board,' she said.

'You do?'

'I do, but I need you to stay calm when I tell you. Do you promise?'

Mystified, Leo nodded.

'She had a run-in with Steven when she came in to give you her project summary. He threatened to destroy her career if she took the job. She told me he hurt her shoulder.'

Leo gasped and his face broke into purple blotches of fury.

'That little shit,' he said through clenched teeth. 'If it weren't for the free office, he'd be out on his ear right now.'

'Remember, you promised,' said Kelly.

'I'll deal with him when I've calmed down,' said Leo. 'Get me Sam's number. We need her, and no jumped-up, spoiled, misogynistic brat will stop me hiring her.'

'You must persuade her first. And you can't tell her you know about Steven.'

'Leave it to me,' said Leo. 'Money talks.'

Chapter V

The ringing of the telephone jolted Edward out of an uneasy sleep. He had been dreaming about shooting his shotgun at someone shadowy in a patch of trees. It took him a good ten seconds to work out where he was. The lurid yellow wallpaper triggered his memory, catapulting him into his nightmare present. *How he hated this ghastly place!*

He fumbled for the receiver, struggling to sit up in bed and compose himself. He cleared his throat.

'Beckett.'

'Edward, it's Buffy.'

Edward froze. *Why hadn't he screened the call?* He made it a habit over the past few months as he ducked and dived to avoid his creditors while searching for a new way to fill his coffers. Now he even had to hide from Buffy Harrington, his erstwhile tame banker and snivelling sycophant. The gods hated him. *How galling to have metamorphosed into Mike Morton while Mike had taken his place with the high rollers!*

'Buffy, old chum, you're up bright and early. How are you doing?'

'Not bad. How are you getting on with business and so on?'

Buffy's voice trailed off. Edward despised the man as a weakling, but he had lost most of his power over him now that Buffy knew his secrets.

'Oh, working on a new project,' he lied. 'It's looking fantastic.'

'A new project? That's great. I presume you'll be able to sort out our little problem soon.'

Edward could hear him panting like an overweight Labrador.

'Naturally. You don't think I would break my word, do you?'

A challenge which Buffy could not take.

'No, of course not. Just wondering.'

'I'm well aware that we need to replace the money in the trust before Hunter finds out. You can count on me, Buffy, as one old Etonian to another.'

Ron Hunter, Buffy's boss, came from a new breed of banker. He did not attend a public school, and had no interest in people like Edward Beckett unless they possessed the money to go with their class. The Old Boy Network disgusted him because they treated him with scorn. Hunter took every opportunity to get his revenge, and he had Edward in his sights.

'I never doubted you,' stammered Buffy.

Edward smiled. Dominance restored.

'Got to get on,' he said. 'No rest for the wicked, eh? Toodle pip.'

He hung up before Buffy could manage a reply, a bead of sweat lodged in his eyebrow and threatened to slide into his eye. He brushed it off with impatience. The nightmare had only just started. How could he extricate himself before the walls caved in? The only option left was to crawl to Mike Morton for a loan.

Mike would give him a hard time and humiliate him, but he would lend him the money. He shuddered.

No way would he lower himself to that.

He drew his knees up to his chest and hugged them. The telephone rang again. Probably Buffy with some lame excuse about forgetting to tell him something. He considered ignoring it but answered just in case. He grabbed the receiver.

'What now?'

'Edward? You're a hard man to get hold of.'

Henri Kanté's silky voice tickled Edward's ear.

'Henri? I apologise for my rudeness. A prank caller has been bothering me this morning. It's been a long time since we last talked. How did you get my number?'

'Your delightful wife, or should I say ex-wife, gave it to me.'

Henri Kanté ruled the roost in Kandar, West Africa. He had the ear of the president and a finger in every financial pie in the country. Edward went to Eton with him and they kept in contact over the years. Edward had avoided doing business with Kanté as his reputation was unsavoury, but Kanté always had a lucrative deal up his sleeve, and Edward needed that money fast.

Hardly daring to believe, he fought to keep the excitement out of his voice as he took a deep breath and forced out his familiar oily tone.

'Most decidedly ex. What's new with you, Henri?'

'I've got a special project in Kandar and I wanted to run it by you. I need investors and your reputation put you at the top of my list.'

Edward pumped his fist in the air and took a deep breath.

'Really? That's flattering. I presume you have vetted it.'

'Naturally, my friend. You know me, always on the level, with you at least.'

Henri's deep chuckle echoed down the line.

'There's one small insect in the ointment but it shouldn't trouble us.'

Edward snorted.

'I should've guessed there'd be a catch.'

'Don't get me wrong. It's a wonderful project with complete databases. All I'm saying is, don't keep your shares too long. Make a profit and get out clean before it's too late to do so.'

'Let me review it and I'll see what I can do. How much is the investment?' said Edward.

'Twenty million pounds.'

Edward's chest tightened, and he swallowed.

'What will they use the money for?'

'Some acquaintances of mine have discovered a new gold terrain north of the capital, Haribar. They need the money for a large-scale exploration of the concession leading to a preliminary resource calculation. Can you raise that much?'

'Is the Pope a Catholic? What do you take me for? I'm divorced not incapacitated. When do you need the money?'

'For the next quarter, after the rainy season. I can send you the report in a couple of weeks. They are just drawing up the final maps and charts.'

'What's my cut of the investment?'

Henri Kanté sniffed.

'Three per cent.'

'I want five.'

'Let's say four.'

The finality in his voice alerted Edward that he should close the deal before Henri rang somebody else.

'Four it is then. I have a new brokerage in Mayfair and we are looking for a suitable project to offer our clients. If I can get my partner, Leo Giustra, to latch on, my son Steven will do the rest.'

'And how is the secret bastard?'

'Not so secret any more. Why do you think Ophelia left me?'

'Let that be a lesson to you. Don't go dipping your quill in strange ink.'

A click in his ear told Edward that Kanté had hung up. He flushed with triumph and lay back on the pillows rubbing his hands. Just when he thought all doors were closed, a new one opened. A successful raise could bring him right back to the centre of things financial, and the eight hundred thousand commission would cover his debts and enable him to buy a decent apartment. The only tricky part would be to persuade Buffy to wait for his money. A nice lunch in the Bistrot should fix that. He picked up the phone and dialled the bank's number.

Chapter VI

Sam slipped out of her parents' house and crossed the road to the park. An early morning mist hung over the trees dimming the bright splendour of their autumn colours. Most trees still clung onto their leaves like mothers to their children on the first day of kindergarten. A few had escaped and lay on the floor in damp abandon, making the paths look like slippery patchwork quilts.

Normally, Sam would stoop to pick up the brightest of them, but she strode along, her head hunched into the high neck of her favourite blue anorak bought for a trip to Siberia and capable of keeping her warm in any weather that Britain could dish up. A cold north wind bit her face and hands but she hardly felt it as she reached her favourite bench where she sat at one end wrapped in misery.

She had been so excited when Leo had offered her the position in Resource Ventures. It had appeared like a new beginning after her failure to get any other interviews. Despite her misgivings about the scruffy office, she had found kindred spirits in Leo and Kelly. Steven had taken that away from her with his vicious reaction. *Had she been too hasty turning it down?* She might have dealt with him given time.

A robin landed on a bare branch in front of her, his chest fluffed out against the cold. He burst into song, daring his rivals to approach his territory. She couldn't help smiling at his bravado but it did not lift her mood for long. She lowered her head to her chest, fighting the sobs that arose there.

The sharp sound of heels clipping along the path made her raise it again. A familiar figure in a quilted coat with fur protruding from the hood approached her bench. Her sister Hannah sat down close beside her, linking her arm around Sam's for warmth.

'Mummy said you'd be out here,' she said. 'You must be nuts. It's bloody freezing.'

'It is a little fresh,' said Sam.

'Are you going to tell me about it?' said Hannah.

'There's nothing to tell. I got offered the job, but I had to turn it down.'

'Why on earth did you do that?'

'I had an unpleasant encounter with the other analyst. He threatened me with trouble if I took the job,' said Sam, sniffing.

Hannah turned to her, eyes wide.

'He did what? I hope you told him to get lost.'

Sam shook her head. Tears sprang to her eyes.

'Honestly, I can't understand why you let him get away with it,' said Hannah. 'After all you've been through. You need to stand up for yourself. It's now or never.'

'It's too late now. Anyway, I don't possess a suit any more. The zip broke, and it tore the material so I can't fix it. You were right about the cooking. I'm sorry.'

'For God's sake, do you really imagine I mind? That old thing was destined for Oxfam before you borrowed it. You have other skirts you can wear.'

Sam sighed.

'I don't know if I'll get another opportunity. I'm a bit long in the tooth for this business.'

'Don't be ridiculous. The more experience you have in mining, the better analyst you'll be. You just need the right opportunity,' said Hannah. 'I won't tolerate any more of this self-pity from you.'

Her cross tone made them both laugh. Sam squeezed her arm.

'Want a cup of tea?' she said. 'Mummy made a coffee cake yesterday.'

'First sensible thing you've said today. Come on. Let's go home. I can help you revise your resume and make sure you're making the most of your experience if you like.'

When Hannah had left, Sam made herself comfortable in the sitting room and settled down to re-read one of her favourite books by Wilbur Smith. Africa floated off the pages and filled her imagination with familiar sights and smells. She was so absorbed in the book she didn't notice the telephone ringing in the kitchen. Her mother came in wiping her hands on her apron.

'Sam? Get your head out of that book. Leo Giustra's on the phone. He says it's urgent.'

Sam leapt out of the chair, dropping her book on the floor in her haste. She followed her mother into the kitchen and picked up the flour-covered receiver from the sideboard. Her mother nodded encouragingly.

'Hello?'

'Sam, it's Leo. Are you busy? Have you got time for a chat?'

Sam almost reminded him it was Saturday but thought the better of it.

'Yes, I can talk.'

She stared at her mother and signalled to the door. Matilda Harris made a bad job of pretending not to notice, sticking her hands back into the bowl of pastry and kneading it as if her life depended on it. Sam rolled her eyes and sat at the kitchen table trying to keep her elbows out of the flour which dusted the top.

'Kelly told me about Steven,' said Leo.

Sam's face fell, and she rolled her eyes.

'Ah,' she said. 'I guess her promise to be silent as a grave was a bit of an exaggeration.'

Her mother looked up from her bowl, her hands hovering over it. She put her head to one side and knitted her eyebrows. Sam ignored her.

'Look, I can only imagine how much abuse you suffered over the years. Being a female geologist in the early days of your career must have been like going around with a sign on your back saying *kick me*,' said Leo. 'But things are changing. I wouldn't offer you the job in the first place if I wasn't sure you could do it.'

'It's not you I'm worried about,' said Sam.

'Kelly is a bit of a chauvinist,' said Leo, the humour in his voice clear.

Sam snorted, blowing flour across the table. Her mother squeaked and leaned so far over to hear what was being said that her chest almost knocked the bowl onto the floor. Sam swung her legs away from the table, trying to distance herself, but the telephone cord wouldn't stretch any further. Why hadn't her parents got a cordless phone yet? It was intolerable. She glared at her mother and put her finger to her lips.

Leo cleared his throat.

'Kelly told me Steven threatened you. He's got a bloody cheek. I'd fire him if it was an option. He's about as much use as a bullock for breeding. He's the price I pay for the office right now. If you come back, we will change that. A few good deals and we can afford to move and leave Steven behind.'

The idea of Steven being dumped was manna from heaven. She hesitated.

'I don't know if I can tolerate him. I just want to do my job without someone harassing me.'

'How many times did you put up with someone like him in the field? At least you can escape here. You can go home every night and every weekend and only see him during office hours.'

'That's true,' said Sam.

'What's he saying?' hissed her mother.

'And have you ever given up on a job because someone bullied you?' said Leo.

'Um, no,' said Sam.

'Why start now?' said Leo.

'But he'll target me and make my life miserable.'

'Only if you let him. You can tolerate him until we can get rid of him. I promise to keep him under control in the office but you've got to show him what you're made of if you want him to back off.'

'I don't know. It's a big decision,' said Sam, stalling for her pride.

Her mother looked as if she would burst, and her distress amused Sam even more than keeping Leo hanging on for an answer.

'I'll raise our offer,' said Leo.

'By how much?' said Sam.

'Five thousand a year.'

'Can I take four weeks holiday?' said Sam.

'No. You can start with three and we'll see how that goes.'

'What about pension contributions?'

'You're taking the piss now. Okay, we can discuss it.'

'When do I start?'

'How's Monday sound?'

'I'll be there. Oh, can you give me an advance?'

Sam's mother, who had been holding her breath with anticipation afraid that Sam would go too far, slumped onto a chair as her daughter smiled wickedly at her. Leo spluttered.

'What's it for?'

'I need a new suit.'

Chapter VII

Sam looked out across the tiled roofs of Mayfair interspersed with the odd concrete monstrosity filling the bombed-out bits like cheap fillings in a row of perfect teeth. Despite her misgivings, she had taken the position at Leo's operation, unable to resist the increased salary and his promises of keeping Steven under control. The recruitment agent had pitched in too, assuring her that working for a small broker would ease her into a City job and give her leeway to make mistakes in a way that joining a massive financial behemoth would not.

Her mother had been furious with her after her telephone conversation with Leo, but only because she came from a generation where *'you took what they offered you without grumbling'*.

'I can't believe she pretended like that. You practically made him beg,' said Matilda later when Sam's father, Bill, arrived home from the office.

'That's my Sam,' her father said. 'The modern world will push you around if you don't fight back. There's no patronage any more. Fight for what you deserve.'

'Well, you're no help,' said Matilda. 'I'm trying to teach her some manners.'

'I'm a bit old for that,' said Sam, laughing. 'Anyway, I got what I asked for and now I have a great new job. I'll be able to move out soon and get my own flat.'

'You don't have to go,' said Matilda.

'You could save a lot more money if you stayed for a while,' said Bill.

A wave of emotion came over Sam and she gave her mother a big hug. For once, Matilda allowed the display of affection and joined in. It made Sam tearful and the sight of her father biting his lip as he watched them made her worse. Sam smiled at the memory and a long sigh escaped her, a sigh without motive, just for the pleasure of emptying her lungs and feeling her chest full of London air.

Since she'd abandoned her field career and come home to work in London, she didn't miss the boarding school food, or the seven-day weeks, the constant local difficulties or drunken ex-pats. Not much anyway. Not yet. *Did professional athletes feel like this when they retired? Had she allowed her career to defeat her?* Guilt mixed with her pleasure at being safe and well-paid in a cushy job in London.

Leo's office did not offer much space for expansion but she had her own office under the eaves. In it she found a shiny new computer sitting on a laminated desk with empty drawers. A comfortable chair welcomed her into its grasp. Despite protesting that she didn't need one, Leo had given her a Nokia 3310 mobile telephone with his number pre-programmed in its contact list.

'You'll wonder how you ever coped without one,' he said.

Kelly had purchased a corkboard which Sam hung on the partition wall separating her from the corridor. Sam populated it with maps and photos of her adventures, mostly to annoy Steven. He had been subdued since she arrived, but she didn't expect that to last long. Resentment emanated from him like a bad cologne as he slunk past her in the corridor. Most of the time, the only evidence that he had been lurking was the trail of blue paper balls he left behind, flicked and missed at the office waste paper baskets and dustbins.

Her blossoming friendship with Kelly turned out to be the best thing about her new job. Sam did not have many women friends because of her years spent in exploration camps around the world, a career that was almost the exclusive territory of men. Kelly's glamorous exterior belied a down-to-earth outlook and a refreshing candour that reminded Sam of Gloria, her best friend, who lived across the Atlantic in Sierramar. Now that Gloria had a second child to bring up, she did not have much time for chatting on the telephone, and Sam had missed having someone to confide in and ask for advice.

Kelly's no-nonsense approach helped Sam through the first weeks in Leo's office and rebuilt her confidence in her abilities to adapt to the new environment. Her deft dismissal of Steven's attempts to belittle her were a template for Sam to follow and she learned fast.

Larger companies had already turned down most of the projects which found their way to Leo's brokerage. Either the deposits were too small to warrant large scale coverage, or they were raising tens of millions rather than hundreds of millions of dollars. Some projects were raising less than a million dollars but Leo considered them all saying 'their second raising will be much bigger and we will be in a prime position if we do the first'.

To Steven's chagrin, it fell to Sam to select the best project for a due diligence visit. There were few to choose from. After an initial read of the candidates, Sam could only find three that met her minimum criteria. To get Steven on side, she gave copies to him for review but she found them in the rubbish bin in the corridor, placed where she would see them.

'So much for détente,' she said to Kelly.

'I wouldn't bother,' said Kelly. 'He's stubborn and stupid, not a great combo.'

After a couple of read-throughs, and a few telephone calls to check on some facts, Sam selected a project in Colombia. This one had real potential if the reports contained accurate information, and she couldn't wait to run a ruler over it. She went in to see Leo, who beamed at her.

'What have you got for me?' said Leo.

'I've selected a project that looks ideal for investment for me to visit,' she said.

'Where is it?'

'Colombia, my back yard,' said Sam.

'Why do you like it?'

'Great geology, easy access near a main road, a good management team. The only way of knowing for sure is to visit.'

'It would be great to offer a project with potential to our investors. They are feeling a bit bruised after the last one.'

'Hardly surprising, but we can improve our offerings by visiting the projects before we take on a client. The upfront costs will be a risk but in the long run we're improving our chances of success,' said Sam.

'I agree. When can you go?'

'As soon as Kelly books my tickets.'

'Don't you mean our tickets?' said Leo.

'Are you coming?' said Sam. 'That'll be fun.'

'I meant you and Steven.'

Sam could not stop her face from falling.

'You want me to take Steven?'

Her incredulous tone made Leo laugh.

'We are stuck with him for now. I need him to improve his due diligence skills, or he can never review projects on the ground without you. The more he learns, the sooner you will be free of him.'

'But he doesn't speak Spanish.'

'You'll just have to translate. Come on. Don't break my balls on this.'

Sam sighed.

'Okay, I'll see what I can do.'

It didn't take Kelly long to sort out the reservations to howls of protest from Steven.

'But we're arriving back in London on Saturday morning, you stupid woman. I don't work at the weekends.'

Kelly raised an eyebrow.

'I'm the one who books your travel and I can organise for you to change flights three times in the middle of the night once you are out there. I suggest you moderate your language or the one who looks stupid won't be me,' she said. 'This is the only flight that fits at such short notice. I'm sure you can ask Leo for some time off instead.'

Steven's mouth dropped open, and he walked off muttering. Kelly winked at Sam, who had observed the whole incident. Sam tried not to laugh, but they ended up giggling.

'He walked straight into that,' said Sam. 'I can't wait to go. It'll be brilliant.'

Chapter VIII

Sam gazed out the window at the lumpy green blanket of treetops below their light aircraft. Her stomach flipped with excitement as they landed on the single runway and bumped their way to the scruffy terminal. Beside her, Steven sighed and threw open his seatbelt.

'Another one-horse town,' he said.

Sam rolled her eyes. *Was he expecting Las Vegas?* It wasn't as if she had been happy about him tagging along on the trip.

The more effort you put in, the sooner he can fly solo, said Leo.

Sam grimaced at the memory and gritted her teeth, poking Steven in the ribs.

'It will be great,' she said. 'Go with the flow in these places.'

The analysts assembled in the grimy terminal building, drinking sweet, strong coffee from small plastic cups. Greg Davis and Ranjit Raja, both from small brokers like Leo's, had joined Sam and Steven on the trip. After saying hello, Sam went to look for a toilet, knowing it might be the last one for a long time. She left them to get acquainted.

'Not a great turn out,' said Greg.

'Only four of us,' said Ranjit. 'They must have been scraping the bottom of the barrel for this one.'

'Three of us,' said Steven. 'Sam's only here as a token woman. She had no qualifications apart from her ability to speak Spanish. My boss's wife is a feminist.'

'Seriously?' said Greg.

'Yeah, but don't tell her you know. She's prickly as a cactus,' said Steven.

By the time Sam returned a subtle change had come over the group, and Steven smirked at her in a way that made her uncomfortable. Not a good sign. *What now? Why had she agreed to his presence on this trip?* She must have been mad.

Their driver arrived and hustled them to a large four-wheel-drive vehicle with three rows of seats.

'Vamos. Tenemos que llegar antes de la caida del sol,' he said.

'What did he say?' said Greg.

'He says we should hurry because we need to be there before nightfall,' said Sam.

They trooped to the car and threw their rucksacks into the back. The driver indicated to Sam that she should sit upfront. She assumed it was so she could translate but he showed no inclination to talk to the others.

'I'm Vicente,' he said in Spanish. 'Where are you from? You speak good Spanish.'

'I'm Sam, from London. I worked in Sierramar for years.'

'The border is nearby. You should visit.'

'Oh, I don't have time on this trip. Next time, perhaps.'

The driver inserted a CD of Latino Rock and drove along tapping his fingers on the dashboard in time to the music.

'Can't you tell him to switch that racket off?' said Steven.

'Rule one of field trips, the driver chooses the music,' said Sam.

They travelled for about four hours through rural countryside. Scrawny livestock and chickens replaced the large herds of plump cattle. Finally, they arrived at a clearing on the outskirts of a forest where a stocky man with a full beard sat waiting on a log.

'You must walk the rest of the way,' said Vicente. 'The road is not suitable for my vehicle.'

'How far is the camp?' said Sam.

'About five kilometres,' said Vicente

'Is the road impassable all the way?'

'I will not go into the forest.'

He crossed his arms over his chest, jaw rigid with refusal.

'Why have we stopped here?' said Greg.

'The driver says the road is impassable,' said Sam. 'We must walk from here.'

'Rubbish,' said Ranjit. 'It looks fine. What's the point of a four-wheel-drive vehicle if it can't drive off-road?'

Sam shrugged. 'It's only five kilometres. We should get there in well under two hours.'

The man who had come out to meet them approached the driver.

'What are we going to do with the woman?' he said. 'We don't have any mules.'

'I don't need a mule,' said Sam. 'I have legs.'

'You speak Spanish? That's good. I'm the camp manager. I'll take you to site. Can the others walk too?'

He focussed on Steven, who sweated in the damp air, his wet shirt sticking to the love handles on his back, and grinned.

'We'll soon find out,' said Sam.

The enforced walk meant a transfer of essentials to a smaller bag for easy carrying. Sam stuffed a couple of t-shirts, her wash-bag and a change of underwear into her small rucksack which already contained her digital camera, a compass, a penknife, a hand lens, a map and a field notebook. She also added some chocolate and hand-held pump for filtering water, one of her father's treasured gadgets lent to her for a field trial. Her waterproof jacket and trousers had to be rolled tight to fit them inside with the zip closed.

She took her walking boots out of her suitcase and changed her socks for a heavier pair before shoving them into the worn leather uppers. The laces creaked but did not snap, as she tightened them and pulled the tongues straight under them. The anticipation of adventure gripped her as she wiggled her toes inside the reassuring footwear.

Picking up her rucksack, she readjusted its contents so that the weight concentrated at the bottom, before transferring it onto her back. She tightened the straps across her hips and shoulders and perched on a log while the others got ready. The other analysts kept most of their gear leaving only their travelling clothes and shoes in the back of the car. Steven did not have a rucksack and carried some belongings in a plastic bag from the duty-free shop. He slipped on some new trainers which looked incongruous on his portly frame. Sam had to bite her lip to prevent herself commenting on the unsuitable footwear. He would find out soon enough. It was lucky they only had to walk five kilometres.

They set out at a brisk pace. Despite narrowing, the dirt road appeared to be more than adequate for vehicles for the first couple of kilometres producing mutters of rebellion from Steven.

'I don't see why he couldn't have driven us this far,' he said.

Sam did not comment but she could see his point. Perhaps Vicente didn't have insurance. Four-wheel drive cars cost a fortune to repair and they probably didn't pay him much. She shrugged.

The forest became thicker, and the road dwindled to a muddy path punctuated by rocks and crossed by tree roots. Sam had years of experience on this sort of terrain and stepped between the obstacles with the agility of a goat. Behind her, the other analysts tripped and slid, their heavy rucksacks making it hard to balance. Steven's face shone crimson with effort and his T-shirt had large damp patches radiating from under his arms. He muttered without ceasing.

'Ridiculous. Just ridiculous.'

Sam smirked. *Serves him right.*

They managed a steady pace despite the tough going but the light faded when thunderclouds gathered overhead making it harder to keep their footing. A sharp exclamation followed a thud behind Sam. She turned around to find Steven lying on the ground, the contents of his plastic bag strewn out to one side. Greying underpants and a bottle of Eau Savage lay at the bottom of a tall tree.

'My ankle,' he said. 'I think it's broken.'

Greg knelt down at his side and, taking Steven's ankle, moved the joint to squeals of protest from its owner.

'It's just twisted,' he said. 'You should be able to walk if we strap it up.'

'You must be bloody joking,' said Steven. 'There's no way I'm walking anywhere.'

His stubborn insistence appeared due more to his apparent exhaustion than to the twisted ankle but there was no way to change his mind.

Sam turned to the camp manager. 'We'll need a stretcher and some torches for the fading light.'

The man sighed.

'Wait here,' he said. 'I'll get one from camp. I'll bring someone with me to help us carry it.'

He set off without a backwards glance and disappeared into the forest. The analysts were alone.

'Where's he going?' said Greg.

'To camp to get the stretcher,' said Sam. 'He wants us to wait here.'

'But it's getting dark,' said Ranjit.

'It's not far. He'll be a lot quicker without us.'

With the help of Greg, Sam helped Steven to sit upright against the trunk of the large tree and gather his possessions. Sam unrolled her waterproof coat and sat on it, eating a square of chocolate and listening to the sounds of the forest, happy in her element. She watched a lizard shin up the trunk of a small tree and snare a cricket. Ranjit lit a cigarette and blew smoke rings which floated up through the trees.

An hour passed without incident before the cracking of a twig alerted Sam to someone's approach. She stood up, assuming the stretcher had arrived, but their guide was nowhere to be seen. Instead, two armed men stood in the forest's gloom, their oily weapons hanging by their sides.

'What the fuck?' said Greg, stumbling to his feet.

Steven whimpered and tried to hide behind the tree. Sam masked her panic and stepped forward.

'Good afternoon,' she said, sticking out her hand in the Latin manner.

The two men looked at each other and laughed, but the smaller one of them shook Sam's hand.

'Good afternoon,' he said, smiling and showing a row of gleaming white teeth. 'I think you're lost.'

'Oh, we're not lost. My companion has sprained his ankle and we're waiting for a stretcher,' said Sam, pretending she talked to men with machine guns every day.

'You must come with us,' said the other man, who was built like a tank.

'Now,' said the first man.

Chapter IX

Steven did not appear to grasp the gravity of the situation and refused to get up and leave with the armed men.

'I can't go with you. My ankle is too sore,' said Steven.

'What did he say?' said the smaller man, poking him with a gun butt.

Steven whimpered but did not get up.

'Leave my friend,' said Sam, in Spanish. 'He can't walk.'

The larger of the men approached Steven and without saying a word, picked him off the ground and slung him over his shoulder in a fireman's lift.

'Put me down,' said Steven, but the man just laughed.

Unwilling to provoke the men, Sam, Ranjit and Greg followed them through the trees. They did not appear to be following a path but their pace did not falter. It was hard to keep up. The group joined another path that followed a stream meandering through the forest. Sam lost all sense of direction as they followed the winding path. The sun had gone in so she had no natural compass. They walked for about ninety minutes.

Sam tried to look on the bright side. If the men intended to kill them, they would have done so already. They might have taken them for ransom, kidnap being a business in Colombia. No wonder Vicente did not want to drive them any further. Local people would all be aware of groups of Narcos in their area.

They arrived at a well-camouflaged camp tucked into the side of a hill. Steven's captor dropped him onto a bench producing a yelp of displeasure.

'Wait here. We'll inform the bosses we brought guests,' said the smaller man and disappeared into the main hut.

'We're fucked,' said Ranjit.

'I don't think so,' said Sam. 'It's likely they'll ask for a ransom.'

'How do you know?' said Greg.

'I've worked many years in Latin America.'

'This is a train wreck,' said Ranjit. 'How long have you been a translator? I bet nothing like this ever happened to you before.'

'A what?' said Sam. 'Where did you get that idea? I'm an analyst. I've worked all over the world as an exploration geologist, and I recently completed a Master's degree in Business Administration.'

'An analyst? But Steven...'

Sam shook her head. The little shit. Steven avoided her glare, pretending to massage his ankle.

'And I've been in a similar situation before, often,' she added.

'I'm sorry. What an idiot you must think me. He told us—'

Before Sam could learn what Steven had said, the door swung open.

'Come in!' someone shouted in Spanish.

Greg helped Steven up and he hobbled into the hut behind Sam and Greg. They peered into the dim room where two bearded men sat at a table smoking. One of them had his feet up on a chair. He wore a pair of hiking boots. Sam screwed up her eyes and stared at the men, a slight feeling of recognition percolating in her brain.

'Who are you, and why are we here?' said Sam.

Her words hung in the air. Had she been too direct? A frisson of fear coursed through her. To her amazement, one man leapt to his feet, his mouth wide in surprise.

'Oh my God, it's Sam,' he said to his companion.

'Sam? I can't believe it.'

The two men raced around the table, grabbing Sam in a sandwich and hugging her so tight her ribs creaked. They both smelled as if they hadn't bathed for days. She wriggled free, relaxed now, trying not to gag.

'Put me down. You don't know where I've been.'

The two men roared with laughter and slapped each other on the back. Greg, who froze to the spot with astonishment, grabbed Sam's arm.

'What the hell is going on?' he said. 'Do you recognise these men?'

'I trained them.'

She saw his expression and grinned.

'No, nothing like that. They were my geologists in Cerro Calvo in Sierramar. They are members of the Torres family, famous 'narco-traficantes' or drug dealers. Guys, this is Marlon and Kennedy.'

'Well, that figures,' said Steven. 'Friends with a pair of drug dealers. You can't trust her.'

Greg and Ranjit shook hands with the men, their relief apparent.

'You're a dark horse,' said Ranjit.

'Don't judge a book by its cover,' said Sam.

'You're telling me?' said Ranjit, but he gave her a warm smile.

'Whisky?' said Marlon.

'Por favor,' said Greg.

The universal language of booze.

'I'm sorry about the mix-up but it's too late to return you today,' said Kennedy. 'We'll put you up and feed you and take you to camp tomorrow.'

Mix-up? That was one way of putting it. Sam beamed anyway.

'What's for dinner?'

A slap-up meal of hearty beef stew and fried cassava chips appeared from the primitive kitchen behind the main house and they tucked in with enthusiasm.

'Wow, this is delicious,' said Sam. 'Maybe I'll stay.'

'Please do,' said Steven, picking at his food as if he expected to find maggots.

Marlon nudged Kennedy, who shot Steven a glance calculated to shut him up.

'You should,' he said. 'My father would love you, and, he's just got divorced again.'

Sam laughed.

'I have enough problems already,' she said, indicating Steven with a flick of her head.

The next morning, Sam woke at dawn and emerged from the shed where temporary beds had been provided for the night. Mist shrouded the trees and beads of dew hung on the massive spider's webs in the bushes. The damp earth emitted an odour of rotting leaves. She did not sleep a wink after noticing several stacks of dynamite in the corner. The scariest sound was that of Steven trying to get his lighter to work.

'I wouldn't do that if I were you. We're surrounded by dynamite.'

Total silence followed by swearing.

'For fuck's sake. This is ridiculous.'

Sam let a long, satisfied breath out into the air. It could have been a nightmare; instead, it turned out to be just another adventure. No doubt Greg and Ranjit would tell some people about their scare with them as the heroes, but she didn't care.

After an enormous breakfast of fried eggs and sweet plantains, Sam waddled over for an embrace from her erstwhile geologists.

'This is not a good project for your company,' said Marlon.

'I hear there are terrorists in the vicinity,' said Kennedy.

'Be safe,' said Sam.

'You should join us. These guys do not appreciate you like we do.'

'It's tempting, but my family would miss me.'

The emotion on parting was real on both sides and Sam couldn't help looking over her shoulder to wink at the cousins and blow a kiss. The same men who kidnapped them brought them to within sight of the exploration camp and left them to walk in alone. Steven's ankle made a miraculous recovery overnight, and he hobbled in under his own steam. They came across the camp manager having a smoke outside the shipping container that served as an office. His eyes bulged when he saw them approach.

'Where the hell have you been?' he said. 'We searched for hours.

'The Narcos took us on a slight detour,' said Sam.

'Los Narcos? How did you get away?'

'It's a long story.'

Despite what seemed like a pointless exercise, the analysts completed the site visit and reviewed the technical information on site. The project showed merit and in any other circumstance would have received a favourable report.

'Except for the kidnapping,' said Greg, as they walked out.

'Ridiculous waste of time,' said Steven. 'Thanks to your friends.'

His ankle no longer seemed to bother him. Perhaps he forgot to limp. Sam shrugged. If he didn't like her before, she couldn't say anything to change that now. The other analysts gave him the cold shoulder since his lies about Sam were exposed, and he made it clear he blamed her. Thank goodness they were going home.

Chapter X

'I think we can agree,' said Ranjit, as they queued at the check-in desk. 'That there would be no point trying to interest the investors in a project surrounded by drug dealers and growers.'

'This project is as dead as a dodo,' said Greg.

'Thanks to Sam,' said Steven.

'You mean for saving our lives?' said Greg. 'You're an ungrateful little shit, Horgan.'

Greg and Ranjit sat together on the flight home but, to Sam's relief, the airline gave Steven an upgrade and he got a seat in first class. He sneered at her as he made his way to the front of the aircraft.

'The cream always rises to the top,' he said. 'Wait until Leo hears about your little friends.'

'It's up to you,' said Sam. 'Are you going to tell him how you faked an ankle injury and got us stranded in the jungle? They would never have found us otherwise.'

Steven did not answer. Sam avoided him at the airport in London, the thought of sharing a taxi being abhorrent. After collecting her baggage, she used the underground to get to her parent's house. She fobbed off their questions about the trip, claiming an intense fatigue, which was close to the truth. She kept secret the revelation about her narrow escape from kidnapping. The Harris family already took a dim view of Sam's forays into dangerous places, having suffered through her previous drama. She would wait a couple of years before letting it slip and then pretend that she had already told them.

Despite Steven's threat to spill the beans to Leo, she couldn't find anything to worry about. He would be sure to tell Leo a distorted version of the trip, but she trusted Leo to ask her for any explanations he needed.

As she had expected, Steven arrived to work before her and headed straight into Leo's office.

'Get rid of that woman,' he said. 'She almost got us killed.'

Leo, who had fielded a weekend call from Greg, had already heard a different version of the story. He raised an eyebrow and tried not to look bored. He couldn't wait to get rid of Steven and his nasty attitude.

'What makes you say that?' he said.

'Her friends kidnapped us and took us to a drug dealer's camp. They might have killed us,' said Steven.

'That's terrible,' said Leo. 'You must have been terrified.'

'I thought we were going to die, but it turned out Sam had worked with them in Sierramar. She was laughing and joking with them as if nothing had happened. It was a mistake to hire her. She's a liability.'

Leo nodded and raised his eyes to Steven's indignant face.

'It sounds like it,' he said, sipping his coffee and furrowing his brow. He paused, his hand in his chin, waving his pen in the air as if counting up the facts. 'How did you get away?' he said.

'Get away?' said Steven.

'Well, you seem to be back in London with no visible injuries, and you made it onto the flight Kelly booked for you. What happened to the kidnappers?'

Colour rose into Steven's cheeks and he spluttered, looking around for an escape. He checked his watch.

'Wow. Is that the time? I've got a call in two minutes.'

Leo grinned at his misery.

'You can tell me later.'

'Okay, yeah, sure,' said Steven who couldn't leave fast enough, walking into the doorframe in his haste to get away.

When Sam arrived, Leo debriefed her on the trip, having let her know that Greg had already told him most of the details.

'You recognised the kidnappers? That's extraordinary,' he said.

'Quite a coincidence. They are nice lads. It's not their fault they belong to an evil crime family,' said Sam.

Leo guffawed.

'You'd find something good to say about the Nazis,' he said. 'Write me some sort of report and don't mention the drug dealers. I've now got to find something else for the investors.'

Sam puzzled over the report for most of the morning. Her concentration on the task was such that she failed to notice Kelly hovering at her door until a sharp cough got her attention.

'Oh, hi, Kelly. Didn't see you there,' said Sam.

'I need you to do me a favour,' said Kelly.

'Sure,' said Sam, pushing away her keyboard. 'What's up?'

Kelly forced out a smile.

'Please don't kill me,' she said.

'Why would I kill you? Spit it out.'

'There's a mining dinner dance tomorrow, and, I kind of volunteered you.'

'You volunteered me?'

Sam's chest contracted with horror at the thought of forced social congress with strangers.

'I've got this friend, and he needs a partner for the evening. I said you'd go.'

'Without asking me?'

'He's a honey. I met him several years ago.'

'Why don't you go then?'

Kelly pouted.

'Don't be like that. You should get out more. Some hermits have a better social life than you.'

Sam considered fighting back but Kelly was stubborn and she liked to get her own way. It would be pointless.

'Okay. Where do I meet him?'

Kelly squeaked in triumph and clasped her hands under her chin.

'The Honourable Artillery Company at eight o'clock. It's black tie.'

'Black tie? Are you crazy? I don't have a ballgown.'

'What about your sister?'

'I guess so. She's probably got glass slippers and a pumpkin carriage too. What's his name?'

'Brian O'Malley. He's Irish with bright red hair and freckles. You can't miss him.'

'I'll hold you responsible if it all goes pear-shaped.'

'Come on. What's the worst that can happen?'

Chapter XI

Sam fiddled with the top of her dress, lifting her breasts to make them more comfortable. She caught the taxi driver gawking in his rearview mirror.

'Eyes front, please,' she said, flustered.

'Sorry, love, but you look good enough to eat.'

Sam blushed and smoothed out the silk of the ravishing ball gown lent to her by Hannah, who had a fit of hysterical excitement when informed that a strange man had invited Sam to a ball.

'Hardly invited,' said Sam. 'I don't even know him.'

'Who cares? You shall go to the ball, and I will make damn sure everyone knows you are there.'

Hannah had a lot in common with Kelly. Sam wondered if they were the real sisters. She allowed herself to be primped and pampered and stuffed into a sheer green silk dress which showed off her cleavage. Hannah spent hours making Sam's ruler-straight hair curl and spraying it stiff with a bottle of hair spray.

She gazed at her reflection in the mirror. *Damn, I'm glamorous*. She grinned. From geologist to vamp with the help of one sister.

'You're good,' she told Hannah. 'I should rent you out by the hour. I'd make a fortune.'

'You're welcome. Don't forget to have a good time. You never know, he could be the one.'

The one. Huh. They pulled up outside a long building with a marble portico. A fleet of taxis deposited their fares and drove off, diesel engines throbbing. Sam paid the driver and struggled out of the door. She stood up straight and adjusted her shrug, a black lacy affair with green sequins, ignoring the pain from her tight shoes. Hannah's feet were only half a size smaller than hers but this resulted in blisters every time.

'Hello. Are you Sam?'

A handsome, well-built, redhead with freckles undressed her with his eyes. Sam relaxed. *Eat, drink, chat, dance, go home. Simple.*

It didn't take her long to regret it. Brian led her to a table of his colleagues who barely acknowledged the stranger in their midst. He talked about himself for an hour, showing no interest in her and drank glass after glass of wine. By the time they had finished their main course, his slur became so bad, Sam struggled to understand him. He then left the table, disappearing for almost an hour 'circulating' and left her at the table while all the couples were dancing together.

It became embarrassing sitting alone at the large table with people looking at her, and instead of beautiful, she now felt over made up and ridiculous. Just when she had decided to go home, Brian reappeared behind her and put his hand on her breast.

'I suppose a shag is out of the question?' he whispered in her ear.

Sam jumped up in horror spilling her drink and shattering the glass. Everyone turned to stare at her just as he grabbed the back of her head and tried to kiss her.

She kneed him in the balls and he dropped like a stone. Tears of fury sprang to her eyes as she tugged at her shrug which had somehow become entangled in the back of her chair. A woman pointed at her and sniggered. Sam pulled so hard at the shrug that the chair flew onto the floor.

'Can I help?' said a voice. A caramel voice that coated her heart with its warmth in one short sentence.

She spun around as if he had shot her.

'Fergus? What on earth are you doing here?'

'Oh, you know, socialising and having a good time. Are you having some trouble?'

'Nothing I couldn't deal with,' she said, watching Brian writhe on the floor.

'Would you like me to rescue you?'

'Oh God, yes, please get me out of here. I'm dying.'

Fergus grinned.

'You look fabulous. I didn't recognise you without your nun's clothes on.'

Sam couldn't help laughing.

'I scrub up nice,' she said.

'You sure do.'

Fergus bent over and removed the shrug from the chair back, holding it for her to put on. He gave a low, appreciative whistle.

'Would madame like to come outside on the balcony with me?'

'I'm not sure. I've already been stood up by one Irish man tonight.'

But she went with him. They stood in the cool of the evening but heat coursed through Sam's body. She sniffed his familiar odour and a pulse of desire flashed through her. She slipped her arm through his, luxuriating in his closeness. *The one that got away.* They stood looking out over the gardens, the smell of jasmine in the air.

He turned to her, and her arm fell to her side, still warm from his body.

'What are you doing here?' she said.

'Oh, my girlfriend invited me, Aimee. She's French.'

He indicated a young slim girl of about twenty sitting at a table near to the window. She waved at him and blew a kiss. Sam's stomach lurched.

'What about you?'

'Me? Oh, blind date,' she said, trying to smile. 'Blind drunk more like. I'm going home now.'

'Can I get you a taxi? My girlfriend won't mind. She's here with a load of friends from work.'

'No, that's all right. The doorman can do it.'

Fergus lingered, unsure, gazing at her. Sam had the overwhelming urge to kiss him, as the passion she had hidden away escaped its shackles and surged to the surface.

'Do you want to have coffee with me sometime?' he said.

'That would be great. Here's my card.'

He took it and tapped his nose with it, a sparkle in his eye.

'Will you promise not to stand me up again?'

'Cross my heart.'

Chapter XII

The coffee shop hummed with conversation punctuated with the hiss of the coffee machine and the gurgle of steam-heated milk. Sam tried to slow down her heart rate by taking slow breaths at the door as she scanned the faces. His familiar golden mane attracted her attention. He had chosen a corner table, and he watched people going by like a lion watching his prey. She pulled down on her shift dress, conscious of its figure-hugging shape, expecting his hungry glance.

She forced herself to approach him, standing at his table like a waitress until he jumped.

'Sam, how long have you been there? You gave me a fright.'

He gave her a hug which lasted just a little longer than it should have. Sam did not object, rather leaning in and luxuriating in his warmth.

'It's good to see you again,' he said.

Sam wiped the hair from her face, flushed with pleasure.

'You too,' she said. 'I couldn't believe it when you turned up at the ball.'

'We've got to stop meeting like this. Would you like a coffee?'

'A latte, please.'

Sam watched him order the coffees and charm the barista. He hadn't changed. She had relived the days they had spent together in Simbako over and over since she had seen him. The strength of his own passion had spooked him but perhaps things would be different now, despite his girlfriend. *How could a twenty-year-old compete with what Sam offered him?*

Fergus brought the coffee to the table and placed it in front of her without spilling a drop. He sat opposite Sam without speaking, making her shift in her seat as his brown eyes examined her. Heat crept up her back and into her face. He smiled at her discomfort and patted her hand.

'Okay, tell all. What are you doing in London? I never thought I'd see you in a suit,' he said.

'I needed a change, after the hostage thing. I did a master's degree in business administration and took a job with a mining broker.'

'The hostage thing. Oh my God. I'd forgotten about that. You attract trouble.'

'Well, I'm sitting here with you, aren't I?'

He smiled but his eyes darkened.

'Are you going to tell me about it?'

Sam looked away from his piercing gaze.

'Not now. Maybe one day. What are you up to? Why are you in London?'

'I'm writing financial articles about mining companies.'

'Wow, that's quite a change in your career path. Who are you working for?'

'I'm freelance but I've had several pieces published in the *Financial Times*. It's nice to be home most of the time after so many years away.'

'That's amazing. I didn't know you wrote.'

'Neither did I.'

Fergus laughed at his own joke. All the women in the café were gazing at him as he threw back his head. All Sam's old passion surfaced, and she took a chance that he felt the same.

'It's been a while since Simbako and our, um, affair, but I wondered if you wanted to try again?'

'Try what again?'

'Going out with me. We can take it slowly and see what happens…'

She tailed off. Fergus had a bewildered expression on his face. He blinked and swallowed.

'I'm not sure my fiancé would like that.'

Sam's heart dropped to her feet, and she gulped down the lump in her throat. From a knight in shining armour to married in one blink of an eye.

'Your fiancé?' she stuttered. 'That girl you took to the ball is your fiancé?'

'Well, not yet, but I'm planning to marry her.'

'I can't believe it,' she said.

Her voice broke.

'Sam?'

She shook her head, afraid to talk in case she cried. He lifted her chin and looked into her soul. The dam broke. Whether it was the misery of the ghastly blind date or the awful truth that she had lost her soul mate to a girl half her age, Sam wasn't sure.

'You said I was the one,' sobbed Sam. 'You lied to me about needing time. I waited. And now you're marrying a child? What did I do wrong?'

Fergus hesitated, biting his lip. He sighed.

'You're like a shooting star, Sam. You fizz around in a blaze of glory and then you disappear again just when things are getting interesting. I can't wait for you to settle down. I'm ready.'

'Did you ask me if I was?'

She did not wait for the answer, thrusting back her chair and spilling the coffees as she bumped into the table. She threw a napkin on the brown tide and headed for the door.

The next few days were purgatory. No matter how she fought against it, Sam kept replaying the scene over and over in her head. Her computer screen danced in front of her eyes, which filled with tears she wiped away, furious at herself for caring so much. All her secret plans for the big reunion had been obliterated and made her realise how much she had relied on them. She became desperate for something to distract her.

Kelly's attempts to cheer her up only made things worse.

'Don't you understand?' said Sam. 'He's the one. I've lost him.'

'There will be others. What about Brian? You disappeared from the ball. He asked me what happened to you.'

'He doesn't remember? Not surprising, considering he's an alcoholic.'

'He's a drinker. But I wouldn't say—'

'He was drunk before dessert. He grabbed my boob and asked me if I'd like a shag in front of the whole table.'

'Oh.'

Kelly wrung her hands.

'It's not your fault,' said Sam. 'In case you are confused; Brian's the drunk and Fergus is the bastard. Now do you understand why I avoid relationships?'

'I'll make you some tea,' said Kelly.

'That would be nice. And promise me, no more matchmaking, please.'

Chapter XIII

Leo discovered that finding a suitable project to get their teeth into was easier said than done. Having worked in Toronto for most of his career, Leo did not possess many contacts in the London mining sector. He wanted Sam to join the other mining analysts on visits to projects looking for investments, but despite his persuasive negotiating, there never seemed to be room for his analyst. Small broking houses tended to get ignored in favour of brokers perceived to offer better access to cash-rich investors.

Leo convened a meeting in his office for his warring analysts. Sam and Steven sat as far apart as the room would allow. Leo rolled his eyes but did not comment.

'We need to generate some projects for our clients,' said Leo. 'I want you both to attend the mining drinks in the RAF club this afternoon, and do some networking for me. See if you can scare anything out of the bushes. Steven, I want you to introduce Sam to the major players. Come back to the office before you go home and tell me all about it.'

Steven nodded, but his sulky face spoke volumes. Sam viewed networking as a new form of medieval torture for introverts but she nodded too. Here was the distraction she had been craving. There was no point doing things the way she had always done them. It hadn't brought her fame and fortune. *What was the worst thing that could happen?* All she had to do was say hello and go from there.

She returned to her office where she entertained herself reading the Mining Journal until there was a soft knock on the door. Kelly Maguire stood in the doorway holding a cup of tea which steamed up her reading glasses, balanced on a fat file.

'Are you okay?' she said. 'There hasn't been a peep out of you all morning. Leo wanted you to give this a read.'

Sam stood up and reached over to remove the cup, slopping some on the file.

'Whoops. Sorry about that. I don't expect it will affect the contents though. Probably another hole in the ground with a liar standing next to it.'

'This could be the one,' said Kelly.

'Hm. Want lunch? Let's go to the Coach and Horses.'

After Sam and Steven had left for the mining drinks, the telephone rang in Leo's office. Few people possessed his direct number. Most had to go through Kelly who screened people with brutal efficiency to make his day run smoother.

'Hello?'

'I've got a project for you.'

Edward's self-satisfied tone irritated the hell out of him. Leo put his hand over the mouthpiece and rolled his eyes at Kelly, who had appeared at the door. She made the sign for tea with her hands and he nodded gratefully. When she was out of earshot, he took his hand off and spoke.

'How are you, stranger?' he said.

'Fine. You?'

Leo smiled. No small talk then.

'Fine, too. Tell me about this project.'

'It's called Yubou, and it's in Kandar, on the west coast of Africa. My old friend Henri Kanté has offered it to us.'

Who was Henri Kanté? Edward's projects had been a disaster so far, but he needed the office space for now so he exercised tolerance.

'I don't think I know him. Does he work in the City?'

'No, he attended Eton with me. He's an entrepreneur based in West Africa. A successful businessman. I trust his good judgement.'

Leo accepted the implied reprimand for doubting his partner. He altered his tone of voice to enthusiastic.

'It can't be worse than anything I've got on my desk right now. What's so good about this offering?'

'They've done mapping and grab sampling and they drilled two thousand metres of core in the last field season.'

'Have they got any analysis results yet?'

'Yes, and there are several places with rich mineralisation. Some of it is bonanza grade of up to fifty grammes of gold per metre.'

'Where did they send the samples for analysis?'

'Alfred Knight, so the QAQC is impeccable. This project has the pedigree of a winner,' said Edward.

'It sounds interesting. We'll need to do due diligence. Can you bike a copy to the office?'

'I'll do that tomorrow. This is the real deal, Leo.'

'How much do they need?'

'Twenty million.'

'Twenty million? Are they using golden drills?'

'It's an extensive programme. We need to raise the money while the market is open to exploration plays. This cash injection will last five years at least, and will take the project to pre-feasibility or even feasibility if we're lucky.'

'I'll get our new analyst to review it.'

'Sam, isn't it? How's he working out?'

'Oh, you know, early days.'

Leo hadn't informed Edward Sam was female. Edward took a dim view of feminism and had once complained to Leo about a woman geologist cheating him out of a fortune, a story Leo took with a pinch of salt. Edward would find out about Sam soon enough.

'Okay, I'll make a copy and get it sent over to you. This is the one, Leo.'

Edward's voice had become triumphant. Leo did not want to get into a discussion about the other sure things Edward had offered him.

'Great. I'll look forward to it.'

Leo hung up and sighed. He needed Edward's projects like a hole in the head but he wouldn't refuse to give it a once over at least. Anyway, if it didn't come up to snuff, Sam would be frank about its merits. She might be prone to gaffes but he wanted to keep her. He imagined her awkward social skills being tried out at the mining drinks and shuddered. She'd manage somehow. *How much damage could she generate at a drinks party?*

Chapter XIV

The Regency façade of the RAF club stood out from the other buildings on Piccadilly. The marble pillars in the doorway were a fiery red marble like the doors to hell, but inside the building was light and airy.

'Which room are we in?' said Sam, who had noted it down. She tugged Steven's arm. 'We haven't got off on the right foot, but it would be positive for the brokerage if we presented a united front.'

Steven sneered at her attempt to build bridges.

'There is no we,' he said. 'I don't understand what you've done to Leo to make him so blind to your toxic nature, but you're on your own.'

Before she reacted, Steven disappeared up the staircase illuminated by a stained-glass window showing scenes from the Battle of Britain, taking two steps at a time. Frustration almost overwhelmed her. *Why had she bothered?* He couldn't have made it clearer that he despised her. She had only made herself seem weak when he had no intention of introducing her to anyone.

Anyway, everyone would be nervous, but some people were much better at hiding it. She had to learn how to command a room or she would never escape her limited world. There were no monsters upstairs.

They were analysts like her. Maybe Greg and Ranjit would be there. She started up the stairs.

Despite her trepidation, Sam had reason to feel at home on the RAF Club. She climbed the righthand staircase and stopped in front of a portrait showing a man with a handlebar moustache. She had been planning to point him out to Steven but now she felt glad she hadn't. A man following her up the stairs noticed her gazing at the portrait and glanced at her name badge.

'A relative of yours?' he inquired; his voice snide.

'My grandfather,' said Sam.

The man snorted.

'I doubt that very much,' he said. 'I suppose you're a member here too?'

'No, I'm a geologist. I'm a fellow of the Geological Society, down the road at the entrance to the Royal Academy.'

'You don't look like a fellow to me,' he said, raising an eyebrow and leering at her.

Sam ignored him.

'Shall we go up?' she said. 'The drinks are getting cold.'

He sniffed and strode up the stairs towards the function room. Sam took a deep breath and blew it out through inflated cheeks. *Just because there was one wanker outside it, didn't mean the room would be full of them.* She checked her lipstick in a mirror in the hallway and, steeling herself, she stepped into the function room which was full of suited backs in circles like stockades to repel invaders.

A long table on one side groaned with exquisite hors d'oeuvres overlooked by portraits of long-dead heroes gazing down at food they would never taste again. A threadbare silk carpet with deep red whorls and navy trim covered an oak floor which reverberated under the tread of Lobb's and Church's black lace-up brogues. Glasses clinked in greeting and a low hum of gossip exchanged between men trying to learn secrets without giving any away.

Sam couldn't see anyone she recognised. The only other women in the room were wearing white aprons over short black uniforms eliciting admiring glances from the analysts. No one had drunk enough to flirt with them yet. *Why didn't Steven Horgan introduce her to a couple of people?* The success of the brokerage reflected on them all but he had only one winner in mind.

She spotted Steven holding court in one corner, his exaggerated gestures making her suspect he was narrating his heroic role in the Colombian debacle. His plump back repelled her from across the room, while daring her to come closer. Then she recognised Greg in the middle of a bunch of men who were all greeting each other.

She tapped him on the shoulder and he spun around. To her great relief, he grabbed her hand and gave it a vigorous shake.

'Sam, nice to see you. That was some trip, eh? Have you met these reprobates? Chaps, this is Sam Harris.' He hesitated. 'I've forgotten who you work for.'

'Leo Giustra.'

'Giustra? Isn't he the bloke who lost all his clients' money in the Granoro crash in ninety-six?' said one them.

Sam wavered. *What was the protocol for this?* Her presence at this drinks party directly resulted from the loss of faith in junior companies after the crash and the subsequent swathe of redundancies among exploration staff like her. She nodded, embarrassed, and searched for something neutral to say.

A young man with a pink shirt and silver cuff-links saved her bacon, and catapulted her into her fifteen minutes of fame, with one simple question. He had been staring at her for about thirty seconds and drawing his eyebrows together in concentration. He slapped his hand to his forehead and let out a loud yelp, causing people to stop talking and turn their attention on the group.

'You're that Sam Harris. The hostage?'

Sam bit her lip, the blood flooding to her cheeks under her foundation.

'I'm afraid so.'

The young man thumped her on the back, causing her to jettison most of the glass of lukewarm prosecco she had been nursing.

'You're kidding me,' he said, examining her face for doubt. 'Boys, we have a celebrity in our midst!' he shouted, raising his glass to her. A sea of unbelieving faces and hostile eyes looking her up and down, judging her babe-factor and finding her wanting. Backs being turned again. But they would not silence him. He thundered.

'It's Sam Harris, chaps, the geologist who got kidnapped in Tamazia.'

Incredulity spread through the room. Sam spotted Steven with his mouth hanging open, pure hatred etched on his features.

'You? I don't believe it,' said one red-faced man, at the buffet, threatening to burst out of his Saville-Row tailored suit. 'Isn't Sam a man's name? Anyway, no normal woman could survive something like that. You must be a dyke.'

Intimidated by the scrutiny, Sam longed to sink into the floor and disappear, but something in his manner riled her just enough to provoke a reaction.

'I'm not,' she said, looking him up and down with exaggerated care. 'But if you were the only choice, I'd have no problem converting.'

She flushed pink with the exertion of standing up for herself. There was a roar of approval from the now considerable audience.

'She's got you there, Prendergast,' said Greg. 'You always were an insufferable bore.'

The man struggled to manufacture a comeback, but finding himself defeated, he refocused his attention on the buffet, hoovering a trail through the expensive hors d'oeuvres like a plump tornado. The sound of his lips smacking forced Sam to move towards a picture window for refuge.

But she was not alone now. Pin-striped suits bore down on her, filled with men eager to meet the girl who survived being a hostage of MARFO.

'I thought you'd be older,' said one.

'I am,' said Sam, causing another wave of laughter.

She had always been a bit of a clown, and she enjoyed herself, as the only woman in the room who had been a hostage. Adrian Black would have enjoyed the irony, if he hadn't been dead, killed in his bath by a snakebite.

'Did you have to drink your own pee?' said another.

'Only as a chaser.'

Another crescendo of laughter. And just like that, after more than a decade of trying, Sam became one of the lads.

Chapter XV

'She what?' said Leo, his eyeballs bulging as he listened to the gossip being relayed to him on the telephone. 'Oh my God.'

He signalled to Kelly to come in and sit down, which she did, mystified at his expression.

'Yes, yes, I see. Okay, I'll tell you later.'

He placed the receiver back onto the telephone like a man placing a box over a snake. Kelly tilted her head in inquiry.

'Holy crap,' said Leo. 'It's Sam.'

'What's she done?' said Kelly. 'Was she rude to someone important? She hates those drink things. You should have given her time to adjust.'

'No, nothing like that. It's much more astounding. She's the Sam Harris, the one who rebels kidnapped in Tamazia.'

Kelly's hand flew to her mouth.

'I knew I recognised the name. I just never imagined...'

They sat in silence for a moment.

'That poor girl,' said Leo. 'No wonder she's a little odd sometimes. I wonder if I made the right decision taking her on.'

'You did. She's uniquely qualified for this job. I wouldn't call her odd. Antisocial, perhaps, but you can understand why.'

They sat stunned for a while, considering the implications. Kelly got up and poured Leo a whisky. He rarely drank in the office but his genuine shock concerned her.

'Thanks,' he said, swirling the ice cubes around the cut-glass tumbler. 'I needed that.'

The door to the office opened and Sam entered, a dazed expression on her face. Steven, who looked shell shocked, followed her in. He pushed past her, went straight into his office and slammed the door, leaving her standing beside Kelly's desk looking like a startled faun.

Leo gesticulated at her to come in and join them. She stared at him as if she had never seen him before but she walked in and sat down beside Kelly in a chair facing Leo's desk.

'Why didn't you tell me about Tamazia?' said Leo.

Sam gazed at her shoes. She took a ballpoint pen from Leo's desk and unscrewed it, causing it to come apart and the internal spring to shoot into the air landing on the carpet beside her chair. She bent over to retrieve it.

'Leave it.'

Leo's tone brooked no resistance. Sam slid back onto the chair and clasped the armrests, avoiding his concerned glance. Her extreme discomfort showed on her face.

'It wasn't relevant,' she said finally.

Leo rubbed his face with his hands.

'If I'd known you were that Sam Harris—'

'What difference would it have made? I don't want anyone to view me as a freak of some sort. It happened. It's over. I just want to get on with my life.'

Sam's defensive tone filled the office and hung in the air. Kelly put her hand over Sam's and squeezed it. Leo's expression softened.

'It's understandable,' he said. 'I guess I would too. The news took me by surprise, that's all.'

'I'm sorry,' mumbled Sam.

'Are you all right now? Don't you have nightmares?' said Kelly.

'Not often,' said Sam. 'It is more like a bad dream I once had rather than something real.'

'You're a heroine,' said Leo. 'Don't be embarrassed. It's an amazing achievement to have survived like you did.'

'Pure luck,' said Sam. 'Please don't treat me any differently. I couldn't bear it. I came to work here because of the relative anonymity it gave me compared to working at a large company.'

Leo laughed. 'You've got that right. No one has heard of us.'

'I didn't mean, um, sorry.'

'No, don't apologise. Just don't keep things from me. I need to trust you if you are to work here.'

'Okay, but I need a project away from London for a week or two while the fuss dies down.'

'I'm working on it,' said Leo. 'But I'd like you to get out there and get us some attention first. Once we have some decent projects, you can spend as much time as you want away from the office. I'm sure we'll get more offers now that we've got a higher profile, thanks to you. I've got a feeling we will soon receive a better class of projects for you to review.'

While Leo waited for Edward to send him a copy of the project and he puzzled over which projects would most benefit his investors, he took advantage of Sam's newfound notoriety to get exposure for the brokerage. He forced Sam to shuttle around town from posh lunch to star-studded party slowly gaining more recognition until they invited her to social occasions that had nothing to do with mining.

Sam resisted, but Kelly encouraged her to spread her wings while she had the chance.

'This is your fifteen minutes of fame. You must be brave and grab the opportunity with both hands. You can't imagine where this will take you. Anyway, what's the worst that can happen. You have been a hostage for heaven's sake. These social occasions only last a couple of hours and you can leave whenever you want.'

Sam could see the logic and forced herself out onto the circuit. To her amazement, she got asked to do an interview on *Women's Hour* on Radio 4, and following the reaction to it, she made an embarrassed appearance on breakfast television. Talking about her ordeal gave her an attack of migraines but Kelly just dosed her with painkillers and put her back on the horse.

Sam's reaction to the social scene in the City was one of disgust at the excess in every sphere. All around her, the dot-com millionaires bought magnums of champagne with which to soak their peers and used fifty-pound notes to snort cocaine, never daring to admit that the good times had gone. Sam forced herself to join in on the fringes, pushing herself so far outside her comfort zone she almost lost sight of it. It had never occurred to her that pretending to be outgoing and social could become as addictive as the cocaine everyone snorted. She refused to try coke, reasoning that she might like it and get hooked.

One evening she got dragged along to a notorious burlesque club called Madame JoJo's, where the dregs of the dot-com boom were drowning their sorrows. Two intimidating drag queens guarded the entrance, insulting everyone who came in. No one seemed the slightest bit fazed by this behaviour and in fact courted scorn from these dragons.

Drag queens, and transsexuals, most of whom also performed on stage, singing or dancing, staffed the interior. Others worked as barbettes or waitresses. The glass collector, a handsome Spanish man, wore a black leather apron, a spiky S&M collar and a pair of black leather boots. Sam resisted the temptation to touch his bare bottom as he walked past.

While the others drank and leered at the spectacle, Sam watched the pulsating bodies on the dance floor, mesmerised by the noise and the bright colours. They reminded her of a flock of parakeets taking a bath in a jungle pool. One dancer lurched towards her, his familiar bulk damp with sweat, a massive smile lighting up his face. Sam's mouth dropped open.

'Mike?' she said. 'I don't believe it.'

Mike Morton leaned over the balustrade and took her hand, a droll smile on his face.

'Sam Harris, as I live and breathe. I hear you've been getting into all sort of scrapes. You haven't changed a bit.'

'Neither have you.'

But it wasn't true. He had put on a lot of weight and he looked pale and blotchy under the flashing lights. He wore a large gold Rolex on his hairy arm and a chunky gold chain worthy of a rap artist around his neck.

'What are you doing in London?' he said.

'I'm working for a small broker.'

Mike wrinkled his brow.

'Sam in the City. Who'd have thought it? Anyone I've met?'

'Leo Giustra. He's Canadian.'

Mike's eyes opened wide and his mouth dropped open. He muttered something Sam couldn't make out.

'Anything you want to tell me?' she said.

'We need to talk,' said Mike. 'I don't think this is the right venue.'

A young woman in a skin-tight dress materialised at his elbow, tugging his sleeve. The territorial look she directed at Sam told her all she needed to know about her intentions for Mike. He threw his eyes to heaven.

'Gordon Bennett! This woman will be the death of me. Here's my business card. Give me a ring, eh?'

Sam shoved it into her handbag. He mimed the sign of a telephone to her. She nodded and gave him a thumbs up. The young woman pulled him back onto the dance floor. As he left, he turned back to Sam and shouted something at her. It sounded like 'shares' but a round of drinks arrived and by the time she looked around again he had disappeared into the heaving mass of people.

Chapter XVI

'You're sending that woman to Kandar? Are you mad?'

Steven turned purple as he thumped the table.

'Actually, I think it's the sanest thing I've done for ages,' said Leo, not flustered by this display of macho fury.

'I already reviewed the Yubou project. It's as sound as a bell,' said Steven. 'Haven't you read my summary?'

Leo did not ask him how he had already seen the confidential report without being issued a copy. Edward's impatience to get going had made it an obvious move.

'Well, Sam's written me a preliminary report which raises some interesting issues you didn't flag up. There are too many unanswered questions for me to make a decision on this one. I'm sending her to check it out for us.'

'Why don't you send me? I'm the senior analyst.'

Leo smirked. *Only in your eyes, sunshine.*

'Ah, but she's a geologist and can verify the drill data. Also, she speaks French and has African experience.'

Steven blew out his cheeks and tried a new tactic.

'Why don't I go with her? Didn't you want me to learn something new?'

Unlikely.

'While I admire your enthusiasm, we can't afford to send two analysts to Kandar. You can go next time, if we make some money on this one.'

'But it's such a great project. I'll have investors lining up to put their money in it. She might put them off.'

Like father, like son. Edward had also thrown a fit.

'That's what due diligence is for. We have no proof the project exists, never mind whether it's viable or not. Anyone can invent a set of coordinates. She needs to go and establish the veracity of the report.'

'But it's a Muslim country. How do you expect her to cope with that?'

'The place is a tourist trap. It's perfectly safe.'

'And who told you that?'

'My wife. She went on a trip there last year.'

Steven deflated and harrumphed.

'You'll regret it. I resent you employing her full time without consulting me. I would never have agreed to this, this imposition.'

'Read her CV. I'm not aware of any male analysts who are more qualified than her. It's just a trial run for three months. If she fails to impress, we just say thanks, but no thanks. Anyway, Kelly likes her.'

A white lie. Leo had decided from day one that Sam would be a permanent fixture at the broker's office, but Steven calmed down.

'Kelly the Oracle,' he sniffed. 'Oh, well, in that case.'

'Haven't you got something to do? I'm busy here.'

Steven's world had collapsed around his ears. He stood at the window in his office and smoked cigarette after cigarette, flicking the butts out onto the roof with vicious fingers. *How had this stupid woman wormed her way into Leo's good books despite the fiasco in Colombia?* She must be sleeping with him. No one would be interested in that opinionated old bag except for a sap like Leo.

He left work early, slamming the door and ignoring Leo's inquiry about where he was going. Jumping into a taxi, he headed for Edward Beckett's flat. The traffic jams just made him crosser and increased his state of self-pity as the taxi meter ticked upwards. When they arrived, he threw the money at the surprised taxi driver and crossed the pavement.

Resentment coursed through his veins as he mounted the steps to the front door and rang the bell.

A harassed-looking Edward opened the door. His expression did not indicate welcome, but Steven was past caring.

'I have to talk to you,' he said.

'Come in,' he said.

Steven followed Edward Beckett into the sitting room. Edward occupied the only armchair, mixing his whisky with a silver baton which clinked on the cut glass and a single cube of ice. He raised the glass to his lips and surveyed the young man who stood bristling with impatience on the cheap carpet with its orange and yellow diamonds.

Steven was short and plump with a floppy fringe of dirty blonde curls. His full red lips would have looked better on a girl. His mother had the same lips, a prime reason for the slip-up that led to the birth of Steven Horgan twenty-five years before.

Edward searched Steven's face for Beckett features, finding none, but there was something reassuring about the air of arrogant expectation that emanated from his pores. Beckett to the core. No need for a blood test. And he had always wanted a son, a chip off the old block, as clichéd as it seemed.

'What can I do for you?' said Edward.

'That awful Giustra has chosen the other analyst to go to Kandar.'

'I know. He spoke to me yesterday.'

'Yesterday? But—'

'Sam's the man for the job, according to Leo. Speaks French too. How can you disagree?'

Steven looked as if he might explode. He opened his mouth to say something, but no words came out. Edward smirked. He had quoted Leo to get a rise from the young man.

'But she's a woman,' said Steven, playing his trump card. 'An old spinster. How can she be a better choice than me?'

Edward raised an eyebrow.

'Leo didn't tell me that. I thought he had hired a man. What's her name?'

'Sam Harris.'

Edward dropped his glass on the floor. The ice cubes bounced across the floor landing at Steven's feet. He bent down to pick them up.

'Leave them,' said Edward. 'Sit down, for God's sake.'

He kicked the glass across the floor where it rolled into a table leg and broke. The smell of whisky permeated through the air. Steven perched on the edge of the sofa, quivering with anticipation. Edward took a deep breath and released it slowly through his nostrils before he spoke again.

'Sam Harris? Now that's a name I didn't expect to hear again.'

'How did you meet her?'

'That bloody woman screwed up a treasure hunt in Sierramar, years ago. I could have made a fortune.'

'What happened?'

'Her principles got in the way, and she allowed the natives to slip away with it instead of bringing it to us.'

'Us?'

'Mike Morton worked for me then.'

Steven's mouth fell open.

'Isn't he your friend, the one who gave me your address? I heard he made all his money in the dot-com boom.'

Edward sneered.

'Pure luck. He used a shell company we formed years ago.'

'So, you made money too?'

Edward stood up abruptly.

'Does it look like it? I didn't have any shares.'

'But didn't you say, he used your company? What happened to the shares?'

'He bought them from me for a song. I thought his idea hadn't a hope of success. Most of those companies crashed in flames almost as soon as they were formed. It was a fluke.'

Steven struggled with this nugget of information. He had always seen his father as invincible, almost God-like in his ability to spot a good investment.

'But he made a fortune.'

Edward looked as if he might punch him. Steven cowered. Noticing, Edward sneered.

'Yes, and then you turned up uninvited, and my wife divorced me taking everything I had left.'

'I'm sorry,' mumbled Steven, chastened.

Edward relented.

'It's all water under the bridge now. This new project in Kandar will get me back on track, and you too, if you've got any sense.'

Steven hesitated.

'Is the project any good? I mean, is it watertight? I hate to say it, but Sam's like the inquisition, if there's anything wrong with it, she'll find out. She's ruthless.'

'She must have changed since I met her. When we found her in Lindos, she wouldn't say boo to a goose.'

'She's definitely not the woman you met all those years ago. You need to be careful of her. Those drug dealers in Colombia were friends of hers.'

Edward looked startled.

'The ones you escaped from? Why didn't she negotiate something if she knew them?'

Caught in a lie, Steven blushed to the roots of his hair.

'It's a long story,' he mumbled.

Edward sighed.

'I've got some calls to make. Can you see yourself out?'

Steven hesitated.

'Now,' said his father.

When his son had left, Edward ruminated on this development. He tried to conjure up a picture of Sam in his mind but he only remembered an awkward young woman in a cheap cotton dress who ate like a horse and knocked over a glass of beer. Mike had convinced him to take her on as a geologist for their project in Sierramar. Her excellent qualifications and cheap salary made it an easy decision.

What a coincidence she had pitched up on his territory again. Life played some strange tricks on him. He picked up the telephone.

'Leo? It's Edward. Have you got a moment?'

'I'm pretty busy today. Can it wait?' said Leo.

'Not really. It's about that analyst you hired.'

Leo didn't bother to disguise his irritation.

'Has Steven been to see you? He stormed out of here a few hours ago when I told him I had decided to send Sam to Kandar alone.'

'Yes, he's been here. I'm not happy with you lying to me about her,' said Edward.

'What do you mean?'

Edward snorted.

'You let me believe she was a man. Do you realise that Sam Harris is the geologist who cheated me out of a fortune? I would never have let you take her on if I had known who she was.'

'That was a long time ago. She had recently graduated from university. It's possible her inexperience contributed to the incident.'

'But she's dishonest. We don't want someone like that working for us.'

'From what I've witnessed, Sam is almost self-destructive in her honesty. Were you in Sierramar at the time?'

'No, it was my associate Mike Morton.'

A sharp intake of breath.

'Mike Morton? I didn't know you worked with him.'

'It was a long time ago.'

'Sam worked with Mike in Sierramar? From what I've heard, it's far more likely to be one of Mike's cockups rather than Sam's mistake. Have you never considered that?'

'She's the one who let the Indians escape with the treasure. Anyway, I don't want you to hire her. She's trouble.'

Leo sighed.

'The project in Kandar is too complex for Steven, and he doesn't speak French. Anyway, I've booked Sam's tickets already and they're non-refundable. Why don't you give her the benefit of the doubt on this trip? You can judge her by the results.'

'On your head be it,' said Edward. 'Don't say I didn't warn you.'

He hung up the telephone keeping his hand on the receiver while he searched for the piece of paper with Henri Kanté's number on it. All humans had their weak spots. Kanté had an uncanny talent for spotting these. He would have a plan to defeat her.

Chapter XVII

Sam couldn't wait to go to Kandar. The rumour that *the* Sam Harris worked at Leo Giustra's brokerage had spread like wildfire through the City. Companies deluged Leo with requests for his analyst to join jaunts to far-flung places to examine ludicrously over-egged deposits. They didn't care that he hadn't enough clients for all these options. They just wanted to boast that *the* Sam Harris had visited their project.

The attention generated by her unmasking left Sam bewildered.

'I've battled for years for people to take me seriously, and now I'm famous for being a hostage. I did nothing to deserve the adulation. I just sat around waiting for rescue. Why are they so fascinated?' she said.

'Who cares what their motive is? This is our chance to earn loads of money. Both of us need to escape for different reasons. The easiest way to do that is to have cash in the bank. You'll only be famous until the next big thing comes along, or they get bored, whichever is sooner. Look at the dot-com boom. It's up to you to make hay while the sun shines,' said Leo.

Sam's parents shunned the publicity as nonsense although they were proud of their rebellious daughter.

Her sister Hannah did a good imitation of support, but could not disguise her intense jealousy of Sam's newfound celebrity.

'I saw you on television this morning. You should learn to dress better. People will think you are a weirdo,' she said.

'Too late. They already do. Why do you think they're writing articles about me?' said Sam.

'Are you okay with all this attention?'

'Why shouldn't I be?'

'Nothing. It's just that—'

'Just that what? That the spotlight belongs to you? This is my chance to shine.'

'I'm not saying it isn't. I lost my appetite for the spotlight years ago when I had the children. I'm just worried you aren't in control of all this. Shouldn't you get an agent?'

Sam snorted.

'An agent? Are you kidding? Don't worry. It'll die down soon. I'm not Princess Diana.'

But she packed her bag for Kandar with more than her usual enthusiasm double-checking its contents and bringing extra tea bags. She didn't admit it to herself but the faux hostage situation in Colombia had spooked her and she made sure she had enough supplies to last if she had any sort of delay.

Sam travelled out to Haribar, the capital of Kandar, in the business-class cabin of an Air France flight from Paris.

'Leo and Steven travel in business class, so I assume you should too,' said Kelly, handing her the tickets. 'Have a great trip. And good luck. I'm counting on working with you for longer.'

No wonder Leo was running out of money. But if it meant that Steven had to stay at home, then business-class travel felt even better. She lingered over her food and watched with horror as *The Phantom Menace* destroyed the Star Wars franchise on her small screen. She ought to note the danger of sequels and prequels and forge ahead in her new career. Whenever she got on an airplane to evaluate a project, a wanderlust that threatened to disrupt her cosy new life hit her with a longing to break away again.

Her struggles with Steven and other aspects of City life made returning to the field more than tempting. Several recruitment agents had approached her about exploration management positions in exotic lands, and she had found it difficult to turn them down. In theory, she wanted to live a normal life, whatever that was, but in practice, she discovered herself poorly equipped to deal with the subtle politics and nuanced conversations in financial circles.

They flew into the dark African skies under a carpet of stars. A huge yellow moon illuminated the top of the clouds making them resemble a sea of vanilla ice cream. Haribar, the capital, twinkled below them as they approached over a sea littered with small fishing boats illuminated by their deck lighting. The aircraft landed with a thud on the runway and taxied to the terminal over runways decorated in swirling patterns of windblown sand.

Sam rubbed mosquito repellent over her arms and ankles and tugged the matching linen shirt over her trousers. She had impregnated her clothes with insect repellent after reading the statistics for death from cerebral malaria in Sub-Saharan Africa. *It would be just my luck to die of malaria after all the adventures*

I've survived so far. She watched a blurred scene through the abraded window as they drove the steps up to the aircraft door at a speed which suggested the driver was in a hurry to go home. She braced for impact but none came.

After a long queue in immigration, she collected her luggage and emerged from the terminal into almost complete darkness. The town had suffered a power cut after her flight landed and only torches broke the gloom. People in floor-length robes carrying illegible placards generated eerie shadows. They were not speaking French, but some impenetrable local dialect. She later learned they called it Wolof.

After a few minutes waiting in the dark, rising panic had Sam in its grip. To calm her nerves, she dug out the itinerary Kelly had given her. In true Kelly fashion, it contained every detail about Sam's trip. The Ramada Blue Hotel, that sounded nice. Maybe she should take a taxi?

'Excuse me. Are you Madam Sam?'

A tall, slim young man hovered in front of her, cringing as if he expected a blow. Sam smiled.

'I'm Sam. Just Sam. What's your name?'

'Amdy Ndiaye, Madam. I will be your driver this week.'

'Please don't call me Madam. It makes me sound so old.'

'But we revere the old in Haribar. I like old women.'

Great, now I'm an old woman.

'Trust me, old is not always good. Just call me Sam. Shall we go?'

Amdy's big white smile broke through the gloom.

'Which hotel?'

'The Ramada Blue.'

The hotel perched on the promenade running along the coastal road which led into the city centre. A cool lobby contained a central square with fountains jetting from the floor. *How many guests had succumbed to the temptation of walking right through them after a day in the heat of Kandar?* A polite man at the reception desk apologised as he handed her a long form to fill in while he made a copy of her passport. Amdy had melted back into the night at Sam's suggestion and she stood at the desk while the tiny droplets from the fountains blew onto her face.

Kelly had outdone herself with the hotel. Sam's room had spectacular views of the Atlantic and she stood out on her balcony breathing in air thick with ozone. She quivered with anticipation at getting to know a new country with a different culture, always her favourite part of any trip. She turned on the television to watch the news but noticed that it was past midnight in Kandar and switched it off again, sliding between the crisp cotton sheets.

Chapter XVIII

Mike Morton stood on the steps of Edward Beckett's building, girding himself for the conversation ahead. He had suffered in the past from Edward's view of him as a jumped-up member of the working class, only tolerated for his entertainment value. Now that the balance had tipped in his favour, Edward seemed unable to adjust and treat him as an equal. Money talked but Edward seemed unable to let go of his archaic beliefs in class privilege to listen.

The dot-com boom had made Mike, just when his dreams of making it big were fading after a lifetime of get-rich-quick schemes ending in failure. His contribution to the market explosion was a pet products website which he had the good sense to sell when offered a ridiculous amount of money soon after starting it up.

That windfall led to his present difficulty with Edward, who had let him use an old shell company they owned together but refused to lend him any money. Edward even demanded that Mike pay him for the worthless shares in the empty company. This did not deter Mike, who realised he had a chance to make his own future. He mortgaged his house, without telling his wife, and had gone all in.

Mike was now a wealthy man with a three-storey Victorian terraced house on a square in the East End, something Edward could not compute. *Which annoyed Edward more, the fact that Mike was rich, or that he (Edward) had missed out on the bonanza?* Mike suspected the former but Edward carped about the latter in Mike's presence. He would have liked to slink out of Edward's life and enjoy his new existence, but there remained one pending matter which they needed to sort out. Mike prayed for a quick resolution with minimum rancour.

Bumping into Sam in Madame JoJo's place ranked as an extraordinary coincidence. He hadn't seen her for fourteen years but finding her there struck him as odd as finding a snowflake in a furnace. She appeared pleased to see him which gave him a warm glow. They had not always seen eye to eye in Sierramar, but an adventure shared always creates a bond not enjoyed with other people.

It also reminded him of the debt he owed her for working there. He had always intended to pay her what he owed, but she disappeared off the face of the planet for a decade or more, giving him a good excuse not to bother. He looked up the number of her aunt's house in Chelsea several times, and wondered if he should call but, somehow, he never did.

The door buzzed, and he pushed it open using the sleeve of his coat to avoid touching the grubby handle. The lift clanged against the sides of the shaft, unnerving Mike, who made a mental note to use the stairs on his way out. He arrived at the door of Edward's flat and knocked.

The door opened and Edward stood there in his faded, salmon-pink, corduroy trousers and lemon-yellow V-necked sweater, a cliché in brown Churches, polished to a mirror shine. Only the bags under his eyes and his un-manicured nails spoke of the deterioration in his standards since Ophelia marched out. His face did not radiate welcome. Instead, he rolled his eyes.

'It's you,' he said, sighing and turning his back, leaving the door open behind him.

Mike ignored this display of indifference, and followed Edward into the small sitting room, rubbing his hands as if to warm them, despite the tropical temperature inside.

'How have you been, Edward old mate?'

Edward brindled at the suggestion he might be old, or a mate of Mike.

'I'm fine,' he said. 'No thanks to you.'

Mike looked around noting the thick dust on the tabletop and the mantlepiece, and the dirty glasses littering the room.

'Now, how was I to guess—?

'Oh, shut up. This is all your fault. If it weren't for you putting your foot in it, I'd still be living in Regent's Park with Ophelia.'

'But you told me she knew about Steven. I'm not psychic. The boy approached me and asked me for your address and I gave it to him.'

'Didn't you think it was odd he didn't have my address?'

A good question. That revelation caught Mike off-guard. He gave Steven the address because of a misplaced attempt to right a wrong. The ramifications of his act echoed through the Beckett's marriage, but he didn't feel guilty; Edward had lied to him. If he had told Mike the truth about Steven, none of this would have happened.

'I'm sorry. I've already offered to help you get back on your feet. What more can I do?'

'I don't need your help,' said Edward. 'What do you want now? Why can't you leave me alone?'

Mike looked at him through narrowed eyes.

'Isn't it obvious why I'm here?' he said. 'Sam Harris's back in town and we owe her.'

'Sam Harris? How would I know that?'

'Don't play innocent with me, mate. She's working with Leo Giustra, your business partner. I'm not a total idiot.'

'He only told me it was her a few days ago. I haven't had the time to consider the implications.'

Edward squirmed under Mike's inquiring glance. Mike's brow furrowed.

'The implications? Don't wriggle out of this. You're aware of our debt,' he said.

Edward's eyes narrowed.

'You must be joking. She's the one who cheated us out of the treasure. How can you even consider giving her the money?'

Mike blanched.

'I never said that. Well, I might have, but it's not accurate.'

'There's a surprise. Mike Morton, economical with the truth. Stop the presses.'

'You were so annoyed, I thought you'd stop funding me,' said Mike, colouring.

Edward sighed.

'How should I guess what to believe? You always lied to me.'

'It was complicated.'

'It always is with you. Lord knows why I put up with you so long,' said Edward.

'I'll admit it hasn't been easy,' said Mike. 'But I offered to let you invest in my pet food company and you laughed in my face. I only wanted to pay you back for all the times you funded me.'

Edward snorted.

'You know it's true,' said Mike. 'I gave you the chance to come in with me and you blew it. That doesn't change the fact that we have unfinished business with Sam. She worked for free for the shares in Sierramar Holdings and we used it as the shell company. She's entitled to her part in the profits.'

Edward raised an inquiring eyebrow and Mike realised that the hole he was digging for himself was getting deeper. He had forgotten he absorbed Sam's salary into his own expenses and she never received it. He placated her with an extra chunk of shares in Sierramar Holdings. Mike blundered on.

'Anyway, it's time to banish the past, and this is the final step. I just need you to sign away the rights to your half of her shares. Then I'll be out of your hair for good.'

Edward sniffed.

'You're not the only one with complications. It's not that simple at my end either.'

'Can't you get your friend Buffy to sort it out. He's the one in charge of the trust, isn't he? Just get him to draw up the papers and contact you when they are ready to sign,' said Mike.

'I'll get on to it as soon as I can.'

'Don't push me, Edward. I've got a new life now, and this is the last thing that connects me to my old one. I need you to sort this out.'

Chapter XIX

The next morning Amdy waited for her in the hotel lobby, his high cheekbones and intelligent eyes highlighted in the blinding morning sunlight. *Wow, he's handsome.*

'Good morning, Madam. I have a package for you from Monsieur Kanté.'

He held out a file box, full to the brim with papers. Sam took the box which leaked sand onto the lobby floor.

'Thank you, Amdy. I'd like to see him tomorrow morning. Can you ask him for a meeting?'

'Oh, he already asked for one with you at ten o'clock. Is that suitable?'

'Yes, that is perfect,' said Sam. 'Can you take me there?'

'I'll be here an hour before. Do you want me to take the box up to your room?'

He reached for the papers but Sam stepped back surprised at the slightly lewd look on his face. Had she imagined it?

'No, that's okay. Thank you.'

'Are you sure you don't need me today?'

'Quite sure. See you tomorrow.'

He nodded and walked off. Sam lifted the box and took it to the lift leaving a trail of sand grains on the lobby floor. She waved an apology to the concierge who appeared with a dustpan and brush to sweep it up. Breakfast was calling, and she had already visualised a plate of scrambled eggs and fresh croissants so she brushed off worries about Amdy's odd behaviour and pressed the button for her floor.

After polishing off her delicious breakfast, Sam returned to her room where she reorganised the furniture so she could sit at her table looking out over the sea while she perused the reports. She read them and wrote comments in her notebook, only getting up to make a cup of tea with the bags she had brought with her. The project had a lot going for it and she could not find any red flags on her first read-through.

She ate a light lunch and went for a walk along the promenade in the blazing heat of midday which soon drove her back to the hotel. After a quick nap, she reread part of the report and wrestled with the maps. It all seemed in order. There was just one thing missing, which she hoped was an oversight rather than a sign of something more sinister. Leo had made it clear how much they needed a successful project to raise the profile of the brokerage.

After an early night, she awoke refreshed and after another epic breakfast, sat in the lobby. Amdy appeared at five to nine and waited for her at the main door.

'Are you ready to go? I'll take you to the city centre to meet Grand Derrière,' he said.

Sam did a double-take.

'What did you say his name was?'

Amdy's eyes opened wide in panic.

'I meant Monsieur Henri Kanté.'

She paused long enough to make him squirm and knitted her eyebrows together in fake confusion.

'Does he have a large arse?'

Amdy snorted and looked at her from under his long black lashes.

'Enormous.'

Sam bit her lip but tears of laughter sprang to her eyes and she laughed out loud, startling the concierge out of his morning reverie.

'The traffic is terrible at this time of the morning. If you would like to, we can visit the lighthouse and stand on the westernmost point in Africa.

'Will we still arrive at Monsieur Kanté's office on time for my meeting?' said Sam.

'The traffic dies down soon. We won't arrive any later.'

'That sounds wonderful. Let's go.'

They crawled along the promenade towards the centre of town as the heat increased and the haze from the pollution rose above the vehicles. After they had driven about a mile, Amdy turned off the main road down a sandy side road towards the ocean. After a few hundred yards they arrived at a short stubby lighthouse surrounded by white walls. A staircase ran around the lighthouse in a spiral to a balcony at the top.

The salt encrusted on the steps made them slippery and Sam struggled to negotiate them in her leather shoes. Amdy had taken off his shoes in a gesture that she had mistaken for reverence and he offered her his arm. Despite being as thin as a whippet, it was like a steel rod and she clung on, grateful. Soon she stood on the iron balcony, its supports rusting under the onslaught of the seawater droplets. She tried not to imagine plunging to the ground in a tangle of iron and stared out to sea.

The Atlantic crashed against the black rocks on the promontory as they stood on the balcony looking out across the ocean. White horses rushed in to the beach and a mixture of seagulls and buzzards squabbled for scraps on the foreshore. Fishermen had pulled highly coloured fishing skiffs up on the shore with seaweed and orange crab legs tangled in their nets.

'How far is Brazil?' said Sam.

'I don't know, Madam Sam.'

'My name is not Madam.'

'It is to me.'

They made their way to Monsieur Kanté's palatial office on the third floor of a new block in the centre of Haribar. Despite a reduction in the number of cars, a power cut had deactivated the traffic lights and chaos reigned in the streets. Amdy drove the jeep through implausibly small spaces to get them to their destination on time.

Sam stepped out of the car into what felt like an inferno compared to the cool autumnal weather in London. Trees lined the pavements but even their welcome shade could not disguise the oven-like heat in the capital. The elevator in the building sat silent despite a noisy generator chugging in the basement, so Sam slogged up the stairs a floor at a time, trying not to overheat and drench her shirt in sweat.

As they entered Kanté's office, she sighed with relief. The temperature must have been twenty degrees lower than in the street. That explained the generator. Monsieur Kanté stood with his back to them, gazing out of the picture window of his office. Chrome and glass furniture littered the floor and copies of Picasso prints decorated the walls. At least she assumed they were copies.

There was no way he paid for this office with income from junior mining projects. And Amdy was right, Kanté had a ginormous arse that distorted the line of his expensive-looking jacket.

Kanté turned around as they entered, sweeping Sam up and down with a practised eye and dismissing her in the same glance.

'Miss Harris. Welcome to Kandar. I hope your journey was satisfactory.'

'Perfect, thank you. You have a lovely view.'

'Yes. I would prefer Paris, but Haribar will have to do for now. Maybe the Yubou project will get me there.'

It was unlikely to be the one in one thousand but you never knew. Sam nodded.

'Save me a space on the Champs-Élysées,' she said.

'I had not expected you to visit. Steven Horgan, your colleague, already knows all about the project. He told me everything had been settled.'

Sam raised an eyebrow.

'Settled? In what way?'

Kanté opened his mouth and then shut it again. He scratched his head.

'I meant organised. The funding, I meant.'

'As far as I know, we haven't decided yet. I expect Steven jumped the gun in his excitement,' said Sam. 'He is inexperienced in these matters.'

She would have said, 'unlike me', but it might get back to him so she just smiled. Kanté stiffened and locked his hands behind his back as if resisting the temptation to strangle her.

'Are you ready for your trip there tomorrow?' he said. 'Amdy will take you. It's a long drive, I'm afraid. They have just started an upgrade to the road but they won't finish it for two years.'

'That's okay. I'm used to uncomfortable journeys. Where will we be staying?'

'There's a serviceable camp on site.'

'Have you been?' said Sam.

Kanté looked annoyed.

'Not yet. I'm kept busy here in Haribar.'

So how did he know what condition the camp was in? Typical laisser-faire attitude. Only geologists and their crews had to live in these places. She made a note to take toilet rolls and wet wipes in case conditions were primitive. Snacks would also be essential in case the food was inedible. Luckily, she had a bacteria-resistant stomach after so many years in the field.

Sam smiled to disguise the nuclear character of the next question.

'I was hoping to pick up copies of the exploration permits and other documents concerning ownership of the area before I left,' she said.

Kanté picked up a paperweight from his desk and examined it before speaking.

'I don't have copies of those papers,' he said.

'That's okay. I don't need them now, but it's part of the due diligence process. I can't write a report without them.'

Not now that she'd got the distinct impression he didn't want her to see them.

'I didn't think you'd need them. I'll see what I can do,' said Kanté, who had retreated behind his desk and was shifting in his chair.

'I'll pick them up when I come back from Yubou.'

Kanté wiped his brow.

'Is there anything else?' he said. 'I have a busy day.'

That was a short meeting.

'No, I'll contact you when we are back,' she said.

'Amdy will take good care of you. He has his instructions.'

There was something sinister about the last phrase but she shrugged it off and shook Kanté's hand. He did not get up from his chair to see them out. Sam and Amdy descended to the street and stepped back into the shimmering heat.

'I need a nice cup of coffee,' said Sam.

'There is a patisserie just up the street.'

They strolled up the pavement, picking their way over dislodged and broken paving stones. Taxi drivers washed their cars under a large baobab tree, whose sparse leaves provided shade from the fierce sunlight. A woman was setting up a small roadside eatery using gas rings balanced on a rickety table. Two large pots teetered on the gas rings, one of rice and another of lamb stew. Piles of red plastic bowls, faded from use, and a box of battered spoons gave testament to the popularity of her cooking.

When they got to the patisserie, Amdy hovered at the door but would not go in with Sam.

'Aren't you coming?' she said.

'I'm the driver,' said Amdy. 'I can't drink coffee with you in there.'

Sam tutted.

'Did you think I would drink coffee by myself?' she said.

Amdy looked at the floor. Sam solved the problem by buying two takeaway coffees which they drank sitting on the sea wall.

'Is Grande Derrière an honest man?' said Sam.

Amdy did not answer.

'He didn't like me asking for those documents,' she ventured.

Amdy snorted and gave her an admiring glance.

'You are dangerous, Madam. You're a rose with hidden thorns.'

Sam laughed.

'You have no idea,' she said.

Chapter XX

The next morning, Sam and Amdy set out for Yubou project just as the sun was rising, avoiding the horrendous traffic jams and dodging the early risers who mostly rode mules or bicycles. Sam pulled on her seat belt and sat with her camera on her lap, tapping her feet with impatience. The long drive ahead of them would only increase her anticipation. Kanté's shifty behaviour had aroused her suspicions about the project and now she could not wait to get there and find out what he was hiding.

The low buildings that lined the suburban streets were often part of compounds with big metal gates. Baobab trees surrounded by traders piling fruit on tables lined the route. As the houses thinned out, they drove along a straight tarmacked road that headed due east into the flat plains of Kandar. Once they had left the suburbs, the landscape was almost devoid of trees. A few scrubby bushes loitered on the sides of the drains running alongside the road and now and then a stand of thorn trees bristled their resistance to the climate.

The further they got from town, the more wildlife appeared, trotting in groggy morning mode across the highway to some unknown breakfast destination. Sam knew just how they felt. The early start and the change of climate had knocked her for six. Families of warthogs, their tails held high, crossed in descending size order followed by swarms of baboons. Entranced, Sam tried to take photographs through the dusty windscreen.

'Wait until we enter the National Park, Madam. It's amazing,' said Amdy.

'When will that be?'

'About seven hours if the road is not too bad.'

Sam's enthusiasm waned after a few hours and dropped further when the tarmac road turned into a gravel one with potholes that could swallow a small car. The remaining traffic weaved in and out of the obstacles crossing into the oncoming lanes and negotiating right-of-way with hand signals and horn blasts. Sam slept, oblivious to the cacophony, strapped into her seat which she tipped back as far as it would go.

Amdy woke her for lunch by brushing her cheek with his hand, a gesture that was oddly intimate.

'This is a good place to eat. The tourists use it on their way to the National Park.'

'Will you eat lunch with me or shall I bring some to you?'

He grinned showing all of his teeth.

'Everyone eats together in this place.'

The restaurant occupied a single-storey wooden building on the side of the road. Aside from two tables of young French tourists, it did not have other clients. Sam and Amdy sat at a corner table with a red-and-white checked table cloth looking over the scruffy backyard where plump chickens pecked at scraps.

'What are you going to eat?' said Sam.

'Thiébou yapp. Rice of meat,' said Amdy. 'It's a local dish of rice and meat cooked with onions and garlic. There is also rice of fish, rice of chicken, rice of peanut.'

'I get the general idea,' said Sam.

She ordered a lasagne, in case the camp cuisine consisted only of rice dishes.

The waitress looked from Amdy to Sam and stared at them as she took their order.

'Why did she look at us like that?' said Sam. 'Is it because I ordered Italian food?'

Amdy squirmed and looked away.

'What?'

'I am embarrassed, Madam.'

'Tell me.'

Amdy fiddled with his cutlery, and folded and unfolded his napkin.

'She thinks we are together,' he said.

'Together? Oh.'

'Many white ladies come to Kandar and find a black boyfriend for their holiday. She thinks you bought me.'

Sam burst out laughing.

'Brilliant. You're my toy boy?'

Amdy nodded.

'Yes, Madam.'

'Have you gone out with a white lady?' said Sam.

'A few.'

Fascinating.

'Why do the young men agree to do this?'

'They get money. And sometimes, a passport.'

'Ah. Now I get it. Don't worry, Amdy. I promise to respect you.'

'I'm not worried. You're beautiful to me. I don't care what the waitress thinks.'

Caught unawares, Sam blushed. Amdy smiled and his face relaxed. He smiled at her and his physical beauty again struck her. He'd have no problem picking up any woman with his fine features and lean elegance.

An awkward silence ensued as she searched for a neutral reply. Then their food arrived and gave them a welcome distraction. They had cooked the lasagne to perfection but Sam could not finish more than half of it. Amdy hoovered up his massive portion of rice and meat and accepted her leftovers. When he had finished, he wiped his mouth and beamed.

'My friends call me Mr Meat because I love meat so much. It is hard for me to afford it for my family.'

'You're married?'

'No, I'm too poor. My mother, uncle, brother- and sister-in-law and her children live with me, and I'm the only one who works. It is difficult to find enough work to feed them all.'

A tired look crossed his features. He might lay it on thick but his need appeared genuine. No wonder he was so thin.

'Why doesn't your brother work?' she said.

'He says he is ill.'

Sam guessed from the tone that Amdy did not believe this, but she didn't comment.

'You're a good man. Allah will reward you with a nice wife soon,' she said.

This seemed to do the trick, and soon she was watching him gobble down a piece of cheesecake. *Poor bugger. Imagine being responsible for your entire family at his age.*

They emerged from the restaurant into the baking heat of midday. A chorus of crickets filled the air with their ferocious, competitive chirping. Amdy had parked the car in the shade under a mango tree but it was still hot to touch. Sam waited for Amdy to unlock it but she heard a yelp of exasperation.

'Madam, we have a flat tyre. I must change it but it shouldn't take me long,' he said.

'Do you need help?' said Sam.

'No, thank you. You should wait in the air conditioning. I'll come and get you when I am ready.'

Sam did not argue. She had not yet acclimatised to the oppressive heat of Kandar so she went back inside and ordered a mint tea. She took out her notebook and reread what she had written the night before making a mental note of the most important things to check in the field. When Amdy appeared at her side after what seemed a short time, she assumed that time had flown because of her concentration on the task.

'That was quick,' she said. 'Are we ready to go?'

'We cannot leave, Madam,' he said, shifting from foot to foot.

'Why not?' she said, puzzled.

'The spare tyre is also flat. I'm so sorry. I made a complete check of the vehicle last night and the tyres were fine.'

'I'm sure it's not your fault,' said Sam. 'These things happen. What can we do now?'

'There is a tyre repair shack about two kilometres down the road. The owner of the restaurant has offered to take me there to get the repairs done. Do you want to come, or will you wait here?'

Sam's instinct was to stay in the restaurant's cool, but she seized the opportunity to take some photographs of the men at work to add to her collection of people from other lands and cultures.

'I'll come. Let's go.'

The owner's car had seen better days but the mechanic's shack was nearby and they arrived without incident. She left them there to go to the local market and buy some fresh tomatoes and onions as she was running low. The mechanic emerged from the shack wiping his greasy mouth with the back of his hand.

'Two punctures?' he said. 'That's unlucky.'

He grabbed one and rolled it over to the tyre spreader and placed it on top. With a few skilful movements, he released the tyre from the rim and pulled out the inner tube. He put his hand inside and felt around until his eyes lit up.

'A nail,' he said, searching on the outside for the head, which he grasped with a pair of pliers, wrenching it out. 'You're lucky the tyre didn't deflate at speed on the open road. You could've had an accident.'

'Why didn't it burst the inner tube?'

'The nail didn't go in straight. It only nicked the tyre after you passed over a bump so it caused a slow puncture instead of a rapid deflation.'

He handed the nail to Sam, who examined it. The nail appeared to be new and had a sharp point. She placed it on a workbench behind her. The mechanic repaired the inner tube with practised skill and speed before replacing it inside the tyre.

'Give me the other one. I'll let this one set before I pump it up with air,' he said.

He followed an identical process with the second tyre and again, felt inside it for the cause of the puncture. His eyes widened in surprise, and he removed his hand shaking his head.

'Now that's a coincidence,' he said. 'I don't think I've ever seen this before.'

He felt the outside of the tyre, finding the correct spot, and pulling out a nail with his pliers, he handed it to Sam. She didn't need to pick up the other nail to know that it was identical. The shiny nail lay in her hand for an instant before she shoved it in her pocket. Amdy had not seen this exchange as he had gone around the back to the shack to relieve himself. Sam kept the discovery to herself for the time being. *What if it was a coincidence?* There was no point worrying him for nothing.

'What was wrong with the tyre?' said Amdy, on his return.

'Oh, just a slow puncture,' said Sam. 'Bad luck, that's all.'

They paid the mechanic and the restaurant owner drove them back to the car park with the two repaired tyres. Amdy had soon replaced one wheel and stored the other under the floor of the jeep and the vehicle ready to go. Sam wrestled with her decision to keep the discovery secret but saw no reason she couldn't tell Amdy later if it became obvious someone had interfered with their trip. She had a shrewd idea who it might be, but since she had no reason to suspect anyone yet, she kept quiet.

Chapter XXI

The horizon threatened to swallow the sun as they came to the end of their drive. It illuminated the creatures crossing the road on their way to their burrows and nesting places. *Noah's Arc would have been fuller if they had built it in Kandar*, thought Sam as she marvelled at the number and variety of wildlife invading the road.

The camp comprised a block-built main bungalow with a corrugated iron roof flanked on each end by two smaller adobe-walled huts with grass roofs. A large mango tree stood in front of the bungalow. A dusty monkey sat among the roots eating a cricket from the head down. Several men were poking at something on the ground with twigs and jumping backwards with high-pitched squeals.

'They've trapped a scorpion,' said Amdy.

Sam jumped out of the car with her camera and approached the group, smiling. On the ground, a large black scorpion cowered from the twigs, its tail raised in self-defence. One man flipped it onto its back where it wiggled in panic until someone else righted it again.

'May I take a photograph?' said Sam.

The men moved back to let her into the circle and she focused on the insect in the dying light of the day.

Satisfied, she moved back again. A man dropped a brick on the creature killing it. Sam winced. Having a seven-inch scorpion wandering around camp wasn't ideal, but she hated the solution.

Dinner comprised a mutton stew and rice. 'Rice of mutton.' The pungent aroma made Sam feel nauseous, but she ate, anyway. Afterwards, she sat outside feeding a banana to the monkey and smoking a cigarette, a habit she had acquired in Sierramar and still continued on field trips. Amdy came and sat near her on the step. Heat radiated from his body.

'Are you married, Sam?' he said.

'No,' she said.

'Do you have any children?'

'No. but I have a niece and a nephew.'

Amdy took in this information.

'Why did your parents not find you a husband? You're beautiful and intelligent.'

Sam smirked. Her mother would have loved to pick her out a suitable man, if Sam had allowed her.

'I'm the one who decides. I didn't want to get married.'

'There's still time.'

'Time won't change my mind.'

'You're not happy, Sam. You need a nice man from Kandar. We know how to make a woman content.'

Sam brindled.

'I've never been happier. Not everyone needs a partner.'

Was that true? She wasn't sure anymore after her encounter with Fergus, but she would not admit to Amdy that she was lonely. She couldn't even admit it to herself.

'I'm off to bed.'

'Goodnight, Sam.'

She slept in a small room at the back of the main house where she hung her mosquito net from pre-existing hooks and bent nails. The heat almost suffocated her and the foam mattress made her sweat rivers into the polyester sheet. She kept a bottle of clean water beside her bed and sipped from it to stay hydrated.

Later that night, Amdy opened the door of her room. His naked body gleamed in the moonlight and, to Sam's half-open eyes, he appeared to be holding a massive stick in his hand. *Was he going to murder her?*

But it wasn't a stick. Sam sat bolt upright in bed and guffawed, half-startled, half-astonished. A conversation she had had in Simbako once came back vividly.

Amdy's poise deserted him and he shrank.

'Why are you laughing at me?'

'Sorry. I didn't mean to laugh. I don't think I could fit that anywhere.'

He perked up.

'We could try.'

'No, we couldn't. I'm not one of those ladies. I'm a professional on a work trip.'

'You don't like me.'

He sat on the end of the bed still holding his member.

'Is it because I am black?' he said.

Sam snorted.

'No. You're a handsome and charming young man, but I already have a boyfriend, and he is super jealous. If he found out you were in my room at night, he would chop you into small pieces and feed you to the crocodiles.'

A white lie, but his silhouette re-inflated.

'You didn't tell me when I asked you before. Can I be your friend?'

'I would like that,' said Sam.

He stood up and loomed over her, planting a kiss on her head. His massive penis bumped against her breasts. No way on earth.

'Goodnight, Amdy.'

'Goodnight, Sam.'

Chapter XXII

'Hello, Edward, it's Henri Kanté here.'

'Kanté, what's up? Has that Harris woman arrived?'

'Been and gone. She's headed up country to look at the project and examine the core.'

'That was quick. I expected her to stay longer in Haribar.'

'She headed out there yesterday.'

'Didn't you meet her? She needs to understand who she is dealing with. I was rather hoping that you would intimidate her.'

'We met at my office. She showed no respect for my position and refused my invitation to dinner. I couldn't wait for her to leave.'

'And here's me imagining your fatal charm would win her over.'

'She's immune to venom. I thought you said she'd be harmless.'

'Apologies, old chap. I assumed she'd be a walkover. Most women her age can't stand up for themselves after their pre-feminist upbringing. However, Miss Harris is not an average woman from that generation.'

'How long have you known her? Didn't you say she'd just started at the brokerage?'

'She had, but I met her years ago. By an amazing coincidence she worked for me in Sierramar in 1987. I had presumed she had got married or been eaten by a crocodile by now. I hadn't realised who we were dealing with until my son told me her surname.'

'Now you tell me,' said Kanté. 'No wonder she didn't seem intimidated by my mild insinuations. We need to take a stronger approach with her.'

'I'm sorry. I had no idea I was launching a cruise missile at the project. The woman is a menace. From what I remember, she's an interfering bitch, incapable of leaving well alone.'

'You're telling me. She asked me lots of questions about the project.'

'What sort of questions?'

'Geological questions about the drilling and sampling and so on. I couldn't answer them. I gave her the reports.'

'Don't worry about that. The samples are legit and the geology is real. It should impress her.'

'But what if she notices?'

'She won't. Did you do as I suggested? The driver?'

'Oh, yes, he's the best there is.'

'So, stop worrying. Middle-aged women like her are desperate for attention. She won't be able to concentrate on the geology once he gets going.'

'You'd better be right. I organised a delay to give him more time to work on her.'

'That sounds interesting. Nothing fatal I hope.'

'Not unless we're lucky.'

'Let me know when she gets back.'

Chapter XXIII

At dawn, Sam swung her legs over the edge of the bed and gave herself a cursory clean with a handful of wet wipes. She smeared herself with high-factor sun cream and selected a long-sleeved linen shirt and linen trousers from her bag. Then she slipped a compact, white umbrella into her rucksack, which she intended to use as a parasol to reflect the worst of the sun.

The route to the Yubou project took them down muddy roads fast turning to quagmires in the seasonal rains which sat in pools and ponds along the track while the surrounding earth dried to dust in the sun. The four-wheel-drive could hardly cope with the mud-filled ruts and the wheels slithered and spun throwing Sam against the door despite her safety belt. New vegetation on the banks spiked the red earth with bright green shoots.

The smell of the red mud reminded Sam of her time in the diamond fields of Simbako, and she allowed herself to remember the short period of bliss she had spent with Fergus. She let out a long sigh of contentment as she recalled the feel of his strong, golden body next to hers under the mosquito net. Those kisses that lasted forever. She hadn't seen him since the fiasco in London but forgetting him had proved impossible.

Amdy had stopped the car, and he stared at her as if he hadn't ever seen her before.

'Sam, are you all right?'

Sam shook herself out of the reverie.

'I'm fine. Just remembering. Have we arrived?'

'Yes, we're here. This is the core storage building.'

He gestured at an old shipping container sitting on the edge of a stand of bamboo which reached skyward in cool greenness next to the dusty walls. A thin old man dressed in ancient overalls crouched under the shade of a zinc overhang. Sam jumped to the ground from the high chassis and stood beside the door of the container as the caretaker removed the lock. The door creaked and groaned on its rusty hinges as he forced it open revealing rows of plastic core boxes sitting in metal shelves along both sides.

Sam asked Amdy to take the boxes out into the sunlight and line them up in order on the ground outside. She filled a spray bottle from one puddle and wet the cores of rock in the first box. There was nothing interesting there, just soil graduating into crumbled rock surface as the hole got deeper. The second box contained weathered rock that had become a mush settled in the rows of the core box. Probably left out in the rain too long.

The third box was more promising. The half-core had held its semi-cylindrical shape and fresh rock gleamed under the wet spray. There were some quartz veins running through it, nothing too exciting but increasing in intensity as the hole deepened. Soon the core showed varied signs of strong mineralisation with large pods of pyrite and chalcopyrite peppering the mineralised areas of the rock.

Sam gazed at the rocks through her lens, comparing the minerals to the written reports she had with her. She took out the list of analyses and looked for the sample corresponding to the mineralised section of core. As expected, the results showed a spike in gold and copper content. She replaced the half-core in the box in the same orientation as it had been when she took it out. It all seemed legitimate and matched the descriptions given by the geologist who had completed the exploration.

She reviewed every fifth box, taking her time, conscious of getting her due diligence correct. Twenty million dollars was hardly chicken feed. Satisfied that the core had given up its secrets, Sam sat in the front seat of the jeep scribbling in her notebook. Amdy helped the caretaker put the core boxes back into the container, and then leaned against the open door smoking a cigarette, waiting for instructions. Sam gave him a thumbs up and indicated that they had finished.

She returned to her summary while they closed up the container and the caretaker accepted his tip. An odd odour like rotting meat percolated into the jeep through Sam's window. She wrinkled up her nose in disgust and looked up from her notebook. The caretaker had locked the container and had left to go to the village for his lunch. The land shimmered with heat but there was no sign of anything that might create a smell like that. Then she saw something move in the bamboo. A lioness was stalking Amdy through the leaves.

A horrified Sam saw the lioness reach the edge of the bamboo and get ready to pounce. She screamed and threw herself out of her chair across the driver's seat and grabbed Amdy around the chest, hauling him into the car. Amdy spotted the lioness as it left the bamboo and grabbed onto the car door as he fell backwards. It slammed shut, narrowly avoiding trapping his legs, which he swung into the car.

The lioness launched herself through the air in the same moment and hit the door with her front paws. The jeep rocked on its shock absorbers as they took the full force of her pounce. She sat on the ground outside the jeep, dazed by the impact and confused by the sudden disappearance of her prey. After a few seconds, she shook herself, slunk back into the bamboo and melted away.

Amdy was still lying back against Sam's chest, his rapid heartbeat palpable. His grey face told Sam all she needed to know about his fright. He grasped her hand which was still clasped across his thin chest.

'You saved me, Madam.'

'It was luck. Her breath gave her away before I saw her.'

'That lion would have eaten me.'

Sam sniffed his dusty afro and patted his chest.

'I doubt it. You're all skin and bone. She would have left you for the vultures.'

'That's not funny.'

Amdy sat up and looked away from her. His reaction confused Sam. She had expected him to laugh.

'I think it is. Are you okay?'

'Just winded, toubab.'

'What's a toubab?'

'That's what we call white people. It means convert in Wolof, our native language. White people came here to convert us.'

'And have I converted you?'

Amdy's face contorted as he struggled with his emotions. Sam waited. Finally, he wiped his nose on his T-shirt and swallowed.

'I'm so sorry,' he said.

'Sorry? For what? I don't understand.'

'Grande Derrière told me to seduce you and take photographs. I took his money. He gave me this camera.'

He tossed a disposable camera onto the dashboard, a sulky expression on his face. 'And now you've saved my life.'

Sam almost laughed. While she found his attention flattering, she had had no intention of getting naked with Amdy. *But where did Kanté get his orders from? It must be Steven Horgan. But why would he bother?* She couldn't understand why he hated her so much. There must be something about this project he didn't want her finding out. Fatal mistake. Curiosity was her middle name.

'I understand your desperation for money,' she said. 'The pressure on you to provide is enormous. I'm just a toubab here from England. Why would you care about me when you have your family to protect?'

'But what about Kanté?'

'I'll deal with him. We'll think of a plan. I promise. Now, let's drive around the concession. I want to see the drill hole sites.'

'Really?'

'Absolutely.'

Amdy wiped his brow with a dirty rag, composing himself before he started the engine. The jeep leapt forward, and they drove from site to site following the coordinates of the drill sites on the GPS across the almost bare plain. A herd of small deer scattered in front of them on skinny legs, some jumping high in the air. At the next site, a warthog family trotted away from an excavation they had been making on the root system of a large bush.

'This is amazing,' said Sam. 'I feel as if I'm on safari.'

'They come from the National Park,' said Amdy.

'Where's the boundary? Isn't there a fence?'

'I don't know. Perhaps they stole the fence to make something else.'

'That figures.'

They visited the rest of the area and Sam finished her review of the geology. There was nothing wrong with the project, except for the possibility it was in an area that prohibited mining. She needed the boundary coordinates to be sure of her thesis.

'Is there an office where I can get details of the National Park?' she said.

'Yes, we pass it on our way back to Haribar.'

'I'd like to stop there tomorrow.'

'We can do that but we will have to wait for it to open.'

'That's okay. I can write up some of my report tomorrow while we wait.'

On their way home, they forded a river with muddy banks and the jeep got stuck in the grey sludge. The wheels spun gaining no traction on the river bed. Amdy jumped out of the jeep.

'Where are you going?' said Sam.

'To get some branches. Wait in the car.'

Sam had no intention of waiting. She jumped out into the mud and slogged her way to dry land. Amdy used a machete to cut large palm fronds, which they shoved under the front and back wheels. Despite all their efforts, the jeep remained mired in the mud. By the time a local man with a tractor had hauled it out, they were both covered from head to toe.

'Take a photograph of me with the disposable camera Kanté gave you,' said Sam.

She posed with her middle finger up.

'Kanté will kill you,' said Amdy.

'I'll be long gone before the photographs get developed.'

Amdy shrugged and took the photograph. They got back into the jeep and drove to camp, their mud covering keeping off the mosquitos as the sun went down.

Another meal of rice of mutton awaited them in camp. Having not eaten since breakfast, Sam ate hers almost as fast as Amdy and they both had second helpings.

'You are now Mrs Meat,' said Amdy, giggling.

Sam wiped her mouth with the back of her hand.

'Mr and Mrs Meat, that's us,' she said. 'Now let's go home and make mincemeat of Grande Derrière and his plans.'

Chapter XXIV

'The coordinates?' said the ranger.

'Yes, of the park boundary,' said Sam.

'We've got a map but I don't have a list of the coordinates. You may get them at the Ministry of the Environment, or the National Parks Directorate, in Haribar.'

He handed Sam a printed leaflet with a small map printed on the back. The scale did not allow for any certainty, but the boundary line ran close to the general area of the concession.

'Thank you.'

'Are you planning on visiting the park?'

'The park visited us yesterday. A lioness charged the car when we were working.'

'Wow! That's unusual. They stay within the confines of the park having learned that humans shoot them outside it.'

'I guess we were just lucky.'

They stopped to eat again in the tourist restaurant. Amdy turned his full-beam charm on and Sam allowed him to flatter and cajole her into buying him a second plate of rice with meat. The owner came over to chat and Sam took advantage to visit the bathroom. By the time she got back, the owner had disappeared again and Amdy had gone out to the car.

Amdy's mood had taken a dive, and he appeared subdued on the way home to Haribar avoiding conversation. Sam left him to his thoughts, presuming he was preoccupied with the problems of feeding his family. Her own whirled around in her head as she considered the implications of her due diligence. Leo Giustra should be pleased with her report but not the conclusions. And as for Steven Horgan…

'Let's drop in on Monsieur Kanté,' said Sam, as they reached Haribar.

'He won't like it,' said Amdy. 'You should be careful of that man.'

'I just want to collect the papers I asked for. I promise not to antagonise him.'

'You don't understand the power the man has over people. When he asks for something, no-one in Kandar can refuse him.'

To Amdy's obvious relief, Henri Kanté had already left the office for the day, and only his assistant sat at her desk reading a pile of papers with an absorbed expression.

'Hello, we're here to see Monsieur Kanté,' said Sam, disturbing her reverie.

The girl jumped and shoved the papers back into a file, dropping some of them onto the floor.

'He's not here,' she said. 'He didn't expect you back today. What do you want?'

'I came to collect the copies of the documents I asked for. Do you know if they are ready?'

'I've got them right here,' said the girl, crimson with embarrassment. She shoved the file she had been reading across the desk at Sam.

'Thank you. Can you tell Monsieur Kanté I collected them, please? Also, I would like to meet him tomorrow afternoon if that's possible.'

The girl picked up a black diary and flipped through the pages.

'Would three o'clock be suitable?'

'Yes, that would be perfect. Thank you.'

'Okay, I…'

The girl wavered but whatever she had been about to say, she had changed her mind.

'See you tomorrow, Madam,' she said.

'Okay, I'm going back to the hotel. I'll call Monsieur Kanté if I need anything else,' said Sam.

Amdy drove Sam to the Radisson Blue and drew up to the main entrance to drop her off.

'Thank you,' said Sam. 'For a memorable trip.'

Amdy looked sullen and did not reply.

'You've been quiet on the way home. Is there something wrong?'

'Why didn't you tell me about the nails?' said Amdy.

'The nails? Oh. How did you—'

'The owner of the restaurant told me. The mechanic is a friend of hers.'

'I thought it was a coincidence. I didn't want to worry you?'

'A coincidence? Nothing that happens around Kanté is unplanned. He's a ruthless man. You just don't get it.'

His vehemence stunned her.

'I'm sorry. I decided based on probabilities. Nothing else happened that we could blame on him. He couldn't have arranged for the lion attack. Maybe you're being paranoid.'

'You don't know him. Kanté is dangerous,' said Amdy. 'There must be something about the project he doesn't want you to know.'

'I'm sure you are right. I promise to be careful. Why don't you go home and get some rest?'

Amdy drove away leaving Sam with a conundrum. Kanté may have tried to sabotage their trip which suggested that Amdy was right. She had to be careful not to antagonise him. She had no contacts in Kandar if Kanté tried any dirty tricks and negotiating the labyrinthine bureaucracy could be made impossible by someone who knew how.

Sam spent the evening reading the documents that Kanté had left for her. They had transferred the exploration concession several times; from a local owner to a defunct exploration company and then again to the company which were developing the deposit. There was nothing suspicious about the transfers. Junior companies were forever swapping deposits and metals between each other and losing them in the down-times.

The documents appeared to be in good standing and she had a full list of the coordinates for its boundaries. The National Park did not get a mention, not necessarily sinister in its absence but she needed to get the coordinates of its boundaries to check her theory. She closed the folder and went to get a gin and tonic at the bar.

***

The next morning, Amdy took Sam into the centre of town before the morning rush hour. They drank a coffee on a bench in a shady square surrounded by government buildings. The Ministry of the

Environment occupied one side of the square and the National Park Directorate the other. Sam headed for the former first; Amdy shook his head and pointed across the square.

'My mother reminded me last night that my cousin Mohammed works for the directorate.'

'Your cousin? Why didn't you tell me?'

'I have dozens of cousins. He is the son of one of my unrelated aunts. I forgot about him. He may be able to help us.'

The marble foyer was almost deserted when they entered its cool interior. A bodge-job wooden partition with a square window sat on one side, at odds with the crafted foyer and its swirling lines and split staircase. Sam approached the window and asked if she could visit the maps department. The official inside the tiny space behind the partition appeared startled to see a toubab in his building, but recovered when she spoke French.

He directed them to the top floor of the building where a small wooden door led into a musty room with a desk at the far end. A young man's ghostly face loomed behind a computer screen. He looked up as they approached and beamed. He stood up to embrace Amdy who slapped him on the back.

'This is my cousin, Mohammed,' said Amdy. 'Sam is here from London. She needs your help.'

'Of course. What do you need?'

All Sam's trepidation about bureaucracy and delays evaporated at his cheery greeting.

'I'm doing due diligence on an exploration license called Yubou, and I need to know if it falls within the boundaries of the Nkolo National Park.'

'An excellent question. Do you have the coordinates?'

'Of the park?'

'No, the concession. I can plot it on here if you like.'

'Really? That would be amazing.'

'I rarely get visitors. It will be nice to have something useful to do for a change.'

Sam copied the coordinates onto a piece of paper and handed it over.

'Would you like a map with the park and your concession on it?' said Mohammed.

'That would be perfect,' said Sam. 'How much does it cost?'

'You can buy me lunch if you like but I don't need you to pay me. It's my job.'

'When will you finish it?'

'Unfortunately, there was a power cut today. The system has gone down and I only have a blank screen. They don't know when they'll be able to restore it, so I doubt I can do it before Monday.'

'I'm supposed to go home tonight,' said Sam. 'I'll call my boss and see if I can change my flight. If I can't stay, will you send it to me instead?'

Mohammed frowned.

'Perhaps, but the file will be enormous. If I have to mail it to you, it might take weeks to arrive.'

'I need the map before then if possible. I'll let you know later today if I can stay longer,' said Sam. 'We'll be here at midday to take you to lunch.'

'Can you bring me a USB stick on which to copy it please?'

'I don't have one with me,' said Sam. 'I think I lost it at Yubou.'

'We can go to the market,' said Amdy. 'They have hundreds there.'

Amdy took Sam back to the hotel so she could telephone the office and speak to Leo. He answered on the first ring.

'Hello, Sam, is that you?'

'Hi, Leo. Were you expecting my call?'

'The telephone display had a weird number on it so I assumed it would be you. How's it going over there?'

'Excellent. I'm almost finished but there is a slight hitch.'

'What sort of hitch?'

'I've been down to the project and reviewed the geology which correlated with the results in the report. I'm convinced that there's a deposit on the site which will benefit from further exploration and has great potential for mining. However—'

'However what?'

'The project area is close to the National Park and the abundant wildlife throughout the project area made me wonder just how close. I am trying to find out where the boundary line is but it will take me a little longer.'

Leo sighed.

'I should have known it was too good to be true.'

'Don't give up yet. I don't know for sure about the Park limits. I could be wrong.'

'What's your plan?'

'We have a contact in the Ministry of the Environment who will get the coordinates for us and combine them with the outline of the concession. That will tell us if the project is totally or partially inside the Park. Maybe only part of the concession is inside the Park, and the deposit itself may be outside the boundary. In that case, they would have to reduce the concession area but it wouldn't be a disaster.'

'How soon can you find out?'

'We can't get the information until Monday, so I would have to stay for another few days. What do you think?'

'What's the alternative?'

'We'd have to wait for the man to post it to us and that might take weeks.'

'You'd better stay on then. I'll get Kelly to change your flights to Monday night.'

'Okay. It's a magnificent project. Let's hope we can salvage most of it.'

'I'll let my associate know. Good work, Sam. Look after yourself out there.'

They returned to the city centre and left the jeep in a private car park while they walked into a street market down a side street. Small stalls lined the road overflowing with random assortments of goods. Sam attracted a good deal of attention from their owners, hopeful of selling her souvenirs and identikit paintings of women with pots on their heads. She cast longing glances at the rolls of wax print material piled high on some barrows.

'Not here, Madame. If you want material, I can take you somewhere much cheaper,' said Amdy, pushing the desperate hawkers to one side.

They arrived at a stall that sold every type of gadget and charger and covers for mobile phones. Amdy shook hands with the young man who owned it. The man pulled a cloth off a section of the stall, revealing a vast collection of USB sticks of all colours and sizes. There were a variety of pouches and holders, some on leather necklaces.

Sam searched through the USBs and chose one which had a gigabit of storage. She then reviewed the pouches and holders. A leather holder with an embossed shield on it depicting a typical local mask drew her eye. She inserted the USB stick, and it fitted perfectly. Amdy took the holder and fastened the leather thong around her neck. It nestled just above her breasts below the line of her shirt.

'Perfect,' said Sam. 'I'll take these. I won't lose the USB if it's hanging from my neck.'

As an afterthought, she picked up another USB of the same size.

'Why do you need two?' said Amdy.

'Just in case the first one doesn't work. They're not expensive and it would be a nuisance to come back again.'

Sam let Amdy bargain for the items watching as the two men laughed and joshed each other before settling on a price. She paid what seemed to be a fair amount to the young man, and they walked back to the car.

Amdy drove back to the National Parks Directorate where they collected Mohammed, who loitered outside on the steps. They found a tourist restaurant where Sam could tolerate the germ level and ate fresh seafood soup with big hunks of fresh baguette.

'Give me your phone number,' said Mohammed. 'I'll text you when I have the map ready. I'll need a USB stick on which to copy it.'

'We just bought two of them in the market,' said Sam. 'I'll leave both of them with you.'

'Do you want a copy on each?'

'Just in case.'

On the way home, Amdy drove with care as the streets narrowed, dodging the moto-taxis with their passengers, mostly women riding side-saddle.

'Is that safe?' said Sam.

'Oh, yes. Some of them carry whole families around. I'm repairing an old motorbike so I can carry people for money. I'm a mechanic so I will keep it well repaired.'

'Would you be able to support your family on the income?'

'Yes. I could get married too.'

'How much would it cost to repair the bike?'

'About one hundred and fifty dollars. I'm supposed to be saving up but at this rate it will take me years.'

He seemed to be waiting for her to say something but Sam ignored his blatant cue by pretending to dig in her bag for something. Amdy put his hand on her arm.

'My mother wants you to come and have lunch with us tomorrow. She is cooking lamb with rice for the whole family. I told her you couldn't come before, but now you are staying perhaps you would like to meet them.'

'Thank her and tell her I would be honoured. Will you pick me up?'

'I have to return the car to Grande Derrière for the weekend. We will need to use taxis from now on. I'll write the address on a piece of paper for you.'

Sam returned to the hotel and reserved her room until the following Monday. Her delayed departure from Kandar did not worry her in the slightest. She had nothing planned in London and the chance to explore the city filled her with excitement. Yet another meal of lamb with rice struck her as a small price to pay for having lunch in a local house and meeting Amdy's mother.

Chapter XXV

The next morning, Sam put on a linen tunic and wrapped a muslin scarf around her head. Unsure of the protocols for visiting someone's house, she asked the concierge to buy an expensive box of chocolates from the local patisserie. He returned with the package, which he gave to her in the lobby.

'Thank you so much. They look exquisite,' said Sam.

'No problem for a beautiful woman like you,' said the concierge with practised charm.

'Can you please ask the taxi driver to take me to this address,' said Sam. 'I'd be grateful if you would tell me how much it should cost too. I don't want to be ripped off.'

The concierge looked at the scrap of paper.

'About five dollars, I should think. I'll tell him not to overcharge you.'

Sam over-tipped the concierge and he gave her a big grin, opening the door of the taxi with a flourish. The taxi driver gave Sam an admiring glance as she slid into the back seat and gave the concierge a thumbs up. Sam had no time to wonder if he planned to overcharge her before they set off towards the Ndiaye residence.

The taxi driver drove along the promenade beside the ocean to a suburb at the start of the dual carriageway that had taken them to Yubou. The traffic had subsided for the weekend and they made rapid progress. Flocks of mixed raptors and vultures lifted themselves off the road as the taxi drove through them. Sam tried to photograph them but mud and dead insects had spattered the windows of the taxi making them opaque.

The car stopped outside a compound with a mud-brick wall and a corrugated iron gate on rusty hinges in a side street parallel to the main road. The driver jumped out and opened the door for Sam. She thanked him and paid him the fare recommended by the concierge. The driver thanked her profusely, and she suspected he had conned her after all.

She looked around her at the quiet streets. Someone had stacked rubbish beside some iron drums acting as bins and bright green liquid leaked out into a pool on the surrounding ground. The stench made her nauseous. A thin dog with advanced mange tottered at the entrance to the compound. He whimpered at her but she had nothing to give him. She made sure not to touch him although her heart broke for the poor creature.

The gate to the compound opened with a creak under her push, and she entered a mud yard which looked freshly swept. Two bungalows occupied the compound, one on either side, both with whitewashed walls and reed roofs. A short woman dressed in a bright coloured dress and matching turban stood in the doorway of the larger house. Her almond eyes gave away her close relationship to Amdy.

He appeared behind her, wearing a coloured kaftan and a small kufi skull cap, and he beamed.

'Hello, Sam. You honour us with your visit. This is my mother, Madame Ndiaye.'

Sam stepped forward for an awkward hug and handed over the chocolates which Madame Ndiaye received with great excitement. The door of the opposite house opened, and a couple came out also dressed in their finery. Sam did not need an introduction to realise that this man must be Amdy's brother. He walked with a cane but otherwise appeared to be in perfect health.

The group filed into Madame Ndiaye's house and sat on cushions laid out around a low central table which had two large pots on it. The reek of mutton assailed Sam's nostrils, and she hoped that she could eat enough to be polite. A plate piled high with flatbreads completed the meal.

Madame Ndiaye served bowls of lamb stew and rice to each person. Sam glanced at the table but could not see any cutlery. She hesitated, unsure how to proceed. Amdy's brother Khaled tore a strip off a flatbread and pinched a piece of meat out of his bowl, soaking the bread with gravy. As she watched everyone did the same, using their right hand only.

Amdy caught her eye and waved his hand at her encouraging her to do the same. She tore off some flatbread and swept it around her bowl before putting it in her mouth. A delicious mixture of herbs and spices infused the lamb stew. She luxuriated in the exotic flavours as she motored through a flatbread and started on another. Madame Ndiaye beamed with pride as she observed the pleasure with which her guest ate.

After eating two bowls of stew, Sam refused a third out of good manners. Khaled passed around a bowl of dates and coconut sweets and then lay along the cushions for a nap. Amdy beckoned Sam out into the yard where he showed her their chickens and a small vegetable patch before opening the door to a shed at the back of the yard.

Sam peered into the gloom. As her eyes adjusted, she noticed a motorbike leaning against the back wall. It had no tyres, and the engine had been partially dismantled.

'This is it,' said Amdy. 'My motorbike.'

He put his hand on her shoulder and wormed his way under the material of her linen tunic. She froze with surprise.

'What are you doing?' she said.

'I need the money to fix my bike,' said Amdy. 'I thought you might give it to me if we make a deal. I'm experienced in giving pleasure to women of your age. I could come back to the hotel with you.'

Shocked by this proposition, cold fury travelled up Sam's spine. She shoved him away.

'How dare you?' she said. 'More to the point, how could you? I thought we were friends. You were just using me. I'd planned to help you but you've changed my mind. You're no better than Kanté.'

'But Sam—'

'I'm going back to the hotel. I don't want to see you again.'

Sam found Madame Ndiaye washing the pots. She thanked her and gave her a hug before letting herself out of the creaking iron gate. As luck would have it, a taxi passed by as she emerged and she flagged it down. She jumped into the back and shut the door just as

Amdy came out looking for her. He shouted her name but she did not acknowledge him, waving the taxi driver on.

On the way home, she tried not to think about the unpleasant incident but it crept into her conscious. She could not blame him. The poverty in which he lived and the situation that trapped him there would make anyone desperate to escape. Although she had turned him down once, they had become close during their trip. *Had she given him hope of changing her mind?*

When they arrived at the hotel, she paid the same fare as the outward journey which cheered her up a little. She made her way to her room, still musing on the Amdy incident. She would give him a day to consider his actions and then have a chat. It was hardly surprising he saw her as a bank when his experience of other white women had been them assuming he sold sex for money.

Also, whether she liked it or not, Sam owed Amdy. He had alerted her to Kanté's scheme and his knowledge about the National Park had put her on the right track as regards the exploration project. If Kanté ever found out about Amdy's betrayal, he would be in danger. She could afford to get him out of Haribar for good for one hundred pounds sterling. It didn't seem a high price.

Early the next morning, she walked across the road to a local bank. Being careful to avoid observers, she took out one hundred and fifty dollars equivalent in Kandari currency which she bundled up and stuffed into the zipped side pocket of her handbag. The suit would have to wait until next month.

Chapter XXVI

Leo waited until Monday before he rang Edward, steeling himself for the expected shit storm.

'Is she back yet? What does the report say?' said Edward.

'Sam should be flying back this evening if everything goes to plan. She gave the project top marks. There are no doubts about the viability of the geology and the potential for a large deposit.'

'That's great news. I expected her to be hypercritical.'

'She's a professional, like I told you. It's her responsibility to make sure the due diligence is carried out carefully, and I owe it to the investors.'

'Can I have a copy of the report?' said Edward.

'I'll send you a copy when I get it tomorrow.'

A lie. Sam had already sent Leo a draft report, but he had no intention of sending it on to Edward until it contained the correct information about the boundaries. Leo did not trust him to wait for confirmation of the facts as he had prior experience of Edward's ability to ignore difficult truths.

'When can we get Steven on the job? Your investors are champing at the bit for this one. I have a few clients that would give their right arms for a slice of the action.'

'They'll have to wait a while longer, I'm afraid.'

'How so? Didn't you say she loved the project?'

'Oh, she does. Unfortunately, there is one piece of data missing that could affect the whole project. She has it in hand but we need to wait until it becomes available.'

'What piece of data?' Edward spluttered. 'I knew it couldn't be simple where that woman is concerned.'

'It's nothing to do with her. She has put in a request for the coordinates of the boundary of the National Park, which is close to the concession, so she can draw it on the maps for full disclosure.'

'The National Park? Are you crazy? What's that got to do with anything?'

'I'd have thought it was obvious. Mining is prohibited inside the National Park. We just have to make sure the concession is outside.'

A sharp intake of breath followed by silence.

'Edward. Are you all right?'

But a dial tone indicated that he had rung off. Leo rolled his eyes and put down the receiver. The shit would hit the fan in Kandar. Thank God the ball wasn't in his court. He glanced up to find Steven leaning against the doorframe.

'Was that my father?'

Leo nodded.

'Did you send him Sam's report?'

'Not yet. I'm waiting for her to send me some last-minute information.'

'What a train wreck! We've got investors lining up and our supposed analyst is having a holiday in Kandar.'

Leo glared at him.

'She's a damn sight more professional than you. That's why she's coming on board full time.'

'For God's sake. You're not really going to take her on, are you? My father worked with her once, and he says she's a criminal,' said Steven.

'I've talked to him about Sam. We agreed to wait for her report on the Kandar project before we make any final decisions.'

'I'm the senior analyst. You can't promote her above me.'

'You were the only analyst, and I never gave you that title. Sam is far better qualified than you. Why don't you take advantage of her experience and learn something instead of complaining?'

Steven pouted.

'I don't understand what you see in her. She rejects our best projects on a whim and she can't even take a bit of friendly banter. Why can't we just hire a man like everyone else? I hate all this feminist crap.'

Leo ignored the reference to banter. He resented Horgan's stone-aged attitudes. Steven was a good fifteen years younger than Leo but centuries behind him where women and their abilities were concerned. Time to put the little shit in his place.

'Ah, yes, the good old days, when men were men, and women were naked,' said Leo. 'She's coming on board whether you like it or not, and if I get the slightest hint that you're bullying her, it will be your arse, not hers. Got it?'

Steven slunk off with his tail between his legs. He slammed the door to his office, knocking paint off the frame.

'What's up with Steven?' said Kelly.

'I've decided to take Sam on full time after her trial period is up. He's not a happy bunny.'

Kelly clapped her hands together.

'I take it you approve?' said Leo.

'One hundred per cent.'

***

Steven slumped into his chair, wheezing with fury. A copy of Sam's report lay on his desk, left there by Kelly who was unaware Leo did not want him to see it yet. Not noticing what it was, he flicked at it with his index finger pushing it to one side of his desk. He tried to concentrate on his Bloomberg screen, staring at it for fifteen minutes but taking nothing in. Exasperated, he picked up the report. *What rubbish had Kelly left for him now?*

His eyes widened as he read the cover page and he looked around as if checking for a trap. The office echoed with the sound of Kelly's high heels clattering into the kitchen, but no one showed the slightest interest in him or what he might be doing. He turned the first page over with the care of someone disarming a landmine and began to read.

Despite his annoyance at having to wait for the report, he couldn't help noticing she had written it well, in precise technical terms with interesting observations about the country and its foibles. All of her comments were positive until the last section: Risks. Here, Sam noted that the information pertaining to the coordinates of the National Park was pending and that the concession appeared to be close or even inside the limit of the park. She advised Leo to hold off on any investment until she got the data because if the concession lay within the National Park, the government would not allow any mining there.

How did she even notice that? Was she psychic? His father would hit the roof.

He opened the window and lit a cigarette. Leo did not allow smoking in the office but Steven could get away with a clandestine cigarette as his office was at the far end of the corridor from Leo's. He stood at the window blowing the smoke into the breeze and enjoying the feel of the sun on his face. The investors were champing at the bit for a good project. There could be no harm in letting them see the report without the bit about the National Park?

He took his Filofax out, the feel of the leather warm on his fingers, and opened the section containing the list of their most reliable investors. He had listed them in order of their total investment appetite so he chose the first one on the list and dialled. The jaundiced voice of their investor came on the line, a man who had almost lost faith in Leo's brokerage after being directed to a series of duff investments. Steven swallowed hard and forced a smile into his tone.

'Hello, mate. I've got a deal for you,' said Steven.

'Is it as good as the other white elephants you dumped on me?'

'Listen, I know we've had some bad luck on a few projects, but this one is special. You'll make it all back on this one. I guarantee it.'

Despite his pessimism, it only took Steven a couple of hours to sell the whole share offering. He totted up the numbers in the notebook on his desk and smirked to himself. He had hit the jackpot with the Kandar project. Their clients, both new and old, would take up almost the whole twenty million dollars. Sam's notoriety turned out to be positive in terms of business, even if her honesty made him nauseous. The new clients had piled into the project like a shoal of piranhas and his commission would be enormous.

Edward would be ecstatic to hear the news of the successful fundraising. Maybe his father could move out of that dive he lived in since the divorce. It had been apocalyptic when Ophelia discovered his existence but hardly his fault. Edward should have told her years ago. Now he possessed everything he ever wanted, a father, a well-paid job and bucket loads of cash. He rubbed his hands together. Happy days.

Chapter XXVII

When Amdy did not turn up to her hotel the next morning, Sam did not dwell on the reasons. She had become apprehensive about Kanté's reaction if he discovered the project could not move forward. The proof she needed waited for her at the National Park's directorate and the sooner she laid hands on it the better. She grabbed the first taxi on the rank and head into the centre.

The usual traffic jams clogged up the streets and slowed progress to a crawl. They were a lot less charming when time was of the essence.

Mohammed looked up as she entered the long dim room and waved a USB stick at her, triumph on his face.

'Tell me,' she said.

'Come to my side of the desk and you can see the map on the screen.'

Sam squeezed past the tall boxes of printed maps and behind the cheap metal desk, standing at Mohammed's shoulder. He clicked on a folder on his desktop and opened a document called *Boundaries*. It took a few seconds to load because of its size. Sam put her hands on her hips and tapped her foot, crossing metaphorical fingers as the image appeared.

It took her another second or two to focus on the image and distinguish the different lines that ran across the topography. Her hand flew to her mouth.

'I knew it,' she said.

'You were right,' said Mohammed. 'Nearly the whole concession is within the boundary of the National Park. As far as I can tell, the area covered by the Park contains all the drill holes.'

'Damn, it's as I feared. This will kill the project stone dead,' said Sam.

'I'm sorry to bring you bad news. Will you lose your investment?' said Mohammed.

'Oh, no, I'm just doing the due diligence. I don't have that sort of money.'

'Whose project is it?'

'A man called Henri Kanté.'

Mohammed became pale. He swung his chair around to face Sam, eyes wide.

'Henri Kanté? I should have known.'

He rubbed the back of his neck and flapped his hands at Sam to go back to the front of the desk.

'Is there something wrong?'

'Yes, no, I didn't know this was his project.'

'Does it matter?'

Mohammed bit his lip.

'I would never have done this work if I had known it was his project. He is a dangerous man and if, as you say, this will destroy his project, he will want revenge.'

A chill rose up Sam's spine. She had assumed Amdy exaggerated when he had spoken about Kanté but real fear showed on Mohammed's face and he had broken out in a cold sweat.

'It's my job to verify the information we're sent,' said Sam. 'Kanté is trying to swindle people out of millions of dollars.'

'And it's my job to give it to you. But I warn you, get out of Kandar today before he finds out you know about the boundary, or it could end badly for all of us. Here.'

Mohammed thrust the two USB sticks at Sam.

'Are you sure?' said Sam.

'I'm sure. But go back to your hotel and check out as soon as you can. Wait in the airport all day if you must, but don't let Kanté find you.'

'What about you?'

'I'll be fine. I had no idea the project belonged to Kanté or I wouldn't have touched it. I still don't.'

'Thank you, Mohammed.'

'Go on, get out of here, and peace be with you.'

Shaken by Mohammed's warning, Sam jumped into a taxi and returned to her hotel. She stopped by at reception and asked them to make up her bill. In the cool air of her room, she tried to still her agitation by folding and packing her clothes into her suitcase. Then she called Leo who picked up at the first ring.

'Hello, stranger. Do you have any news for me?' said Leo.

'It's bad news I'm afraid. My hunch played out. Almost the entire concession is within the National Park boundary.'

Leo sighed.

'Jesus. This is a disaster,' he said at last. She could sense him pacing the office. 'I wish I smoked.'

'At least we haven't sold it to clients yet,' said Sam.

'That's what you think,' said Leo. 'That was Edward, my partner, on the phone congratulating me on raising most of the money for Kandar. I had to disabuse him of the idea that they had cleared the concession for investment.'

'Who told him that? Steven?' said Sam.

'Yes, I suspect the little shit has been hawking the project to our clients.'

Sam took a deep breath.

'Why do you tolerate him?' she said.

'He's Edward's son. That's why I'm so desperate to get some good deals together. I want to sever my attachment to the Beckett family.'

All the hairs stood up on Sam's arms. The past had arrived in the present day.

'Your partner is Edward Beckett?'

'Yes, the financier. Have you come across him before?'

'You could say that. He financed my first contract in Sierramar. Does he know I work here?'

'Would that matter?'

'I don't know. I shouldn't think so. It was a long time ago, and I only met him once.'

'He knows I took on a new analyst, but he's never asked for a name. I'm not sure to be honest.'

'Maybe it's best that way,' said Sam. 'Okay, I'll be on the flight tonight and I'll try to make it into the office in the morning, barring delays.'

'Sam?'

'Yes?'

'You've done a bloody good job out there. We'll tell the investors to hold fire with their money as our analyst has found a problem with the project. They'll be happy we got it right for once. There'll be other projects. Just come home safe and we'll make a plan.'

'Okay, see you tomorrow then.'

Sam hung up. She stood up and walked over the window where she stared at the sea. Edward Beckett. *What a coincidence. Was it possible he held a grudge about the Inca treasure?* The only man who could tell her that had given her his card in a night club. It was time to do some investigating before this got out of hand.

She emptied her handbag onto her bed. There among the pens and USBs and receipts she found Mike Morton's card. She would call him the minute she got back to London. Meanwhile, she searched for the leather thong and carrying case by tipping the contents of her suitcase onto the ground and replacing everything one by one.

Once she had found the pouch, she stuck one of the USB sticks into it and hung it low around her neck so it nestled in her cleavage. She buttoned up her shirt so it hid the necklace and she replaced the other USBs in a side pocket of her handbag. Zipping up her bag, she called down to reception to have someone collect her bag and headed for the lift.

Chapter XXVIII

Henri Kanté's secretary handed the envelope from the Kodak shop to him with a smirk which she attempted to hide.

'Have you looked at these?' said Kanté.

'No, sir,' she said, turning on her heel and exiting his office before he could ask her any awkward questions.

He lit a cigarette and made himself comfortable in a leather chair before flicking open the envelope which seemed light in his hand. He shook it and one solitary photograph fell out, floating to the floor and landing face down on the carpet. Stuck in the squishy leather grasp of his chair, Kanté struggled to bend over to pick it up. He turned it over. A roar of fury shook his body as he focused on the muddy figure with her middle finger in the air posing for the camera.

How dare the Harris woman insult him this way? And where were the photographs of her in flagrante? Amdy had claimed he seduced the woman and took photos of her naked body. Kanté had even slapped Amdy's back when he handed over the disposable camera with the supposed evidence. They would both pay for this.

He strode to the door and flung it open.

'Miss Bemba, get me Amdy by telephone. Now!'

His secretary was nowhere to be seen. She had slipped out on an errand avoiding his fury, and he had wasted his time shouting to an empty room. He swore again and re-entered his office scrabbling in his desk drawer until he pulled out a scrap of paper with Amdy's mobile number on it. *The gigolo was toast.*

Before he could dial Amdy's number, the telephone rang making him jump. Edward Beckett's agitated voice grated on his eardrum.

'Calm down, Edward. I can't understand a word you are saying. Take a deep breath and repeat what you just said at a normal pace.'

'She's found it,' said Edward. 'The fatal flaw.'

'Who's found what?'

'Sam Harris. Her report on your project will state that the concession may be within the boundary of the National Park. That's the slight inconvenience you spoke of, isn't it?'

Kanté sat down heavily, gasping for breath. Finally, he pulled himself together.

'How did she get this information?'

His voice trembled with fury.

'I don't know. She just confirmed the facts to Leo Giustra by telephone. She's got the data on a USB stick,' said Edward. 'It's a bleeding disaster. You told me it shouldn't be a problem.'

'I never imagined she would discover this on such a short trip. There's no way of knowing where the boundary is. I had my men rip up the fences.'

'She must be psychic then. Can we stop her carrying the data to London? Where did she get the data from?' said Edward, his voice breaking.

'She can't do it from London. There must be someone else working with her in Haribar. Did you get his name?'

'Hang on, I'll check my emails. Leo forwarded the information to me. The man's name must be there.'

Kanté lit a cigarette and took deep drags as he tried to quell the panic that assailed him.

'Oh, yes, here it is. The man's name is Mohammed something.'

'That doesn't narrow it down much. They name nearly every firstborn in Kandar Mohammed. Any surname? Which ministry?'

'I don't have a surname. He works at the National Parks Directorate. Sam told me he was a cousin of her driver.'

'That's interesting. It's given me an idea. Don't worry, I have no intention of missing out on twenty million dollars. We'll soon get our investors back.'

'But how are you going to do that? The project is dead.'

'The only thing that's dead will be Amdy Ndiaye, and this fellow will join him if he doesn't cooperate. Leave it with me.'

Edward whimpered.

'This project is make-or-break for me. I'm relying on it.'

'Stop fussing. My fingers are in all the pies around here. I'll deal with our problem at the Park's Directorate. I'll find our driver later. Meanwhile, the timing has just speeded up. Get your son to round up the investors. This must get sewn up fast, so we can get in and out before the truth gets out.

'Isn't that risky? What if the project collapses?'

'Why do you think the timing has changed? Trust me. We can pull this off.'

***

A large silhouette stood in the doorway of his office blocking out the light that entered from the stairwell. Mohammed blinked and screwed up his eyes, but he could not see the man against the light.

'Hello, can I help you?'

Henri Kanté stepped into the room, the sharp creases on his shiny suit catching the light like blades. He brushed an invisible hair off his shoulder and approached Mohammed's desk. His notoriety caused Mohammed to quake as he recognised his visitor. Mohammed adopted an obsequious, fawning manner and did not look his visitor in the eye. Kanté sat opposite him, narrowing his eyes to small slits.

'Monsieur Kanté,' stammered Mohammed. 'To what do I owe the honour of this visit?

'I need you to do me a favour,' he said.

'What sort of favour, Monsieur Kanté?'

'You know who I am?'

'Everyone knows who you are, sir.'

'I understand that you've been working on a project.'

'A project? I don't do private work. The ministry doesn't allow it.'

'Don't lie to me. You've been helping the Harris woman.'

'Yes, that's true, but she didn't pay me anything. I only gave her some coordinates for the park boundary. That's free information.'

'How did she find you?'

'My cousin Amdy drove her to the project. He asked me for help.'

'Did you give her a map?'

'No, I just copied the coordinates onto a USB stick for her. She's taking it out of the country with her.'

'When?'

'I don't know.'

'I don't believe you.'

'Is this a test? I can't lie to a man I've just met. I've just been to the Haj; it would stain my soul.'

'You will tell me for the sake of your family.'

Kanté picked up a framed photograph from Mohammed's desk and stroked the woman pictured with his index finger, a gesture that induced an involuntary shudder from Mohammed.

'That's a pretty wife you've got there. It must have been an arranged marriage. I can't imagine she chose you. Anyway, my men will take her on a trip with your son if you don't do this small favour for me,' said Kanté, leering.

Mohammed swallowed. He could not tolerate the thought of his beloved wife and child in the hands of these thugs. He had only met Sam once. She would need to fend for herself until the flight.

'Will it be the end of the matter? Do you swear never to harm them?'

'That's all I need from you. We can all be friends afterwards, and it will be like nothing ever happened.'

Mohammed sighed.

'She's leaving tonight on the Air France flight. I saw the ticket in her bag.'

Chapter XXIX

Sam drummed her fingers on the desk as the receptionist tried again to use her credit card to pay her bill.

'I'm sorry madam, it won't go through. Don't you have another card?'

The flustered receptionist gave Sam a pleading look as the queue grew behind her.

'I'll call London and see if they can pay from there,' said Sam, moving aside.

She put up her hand and waved the next person to the desk. She took the invoice with her and returned to the lifts which seemed to take an age to arrive. A nasty prickling sensation, which she refused to acknowledge, crept up her back making her feel nauseous. A man stood too close to her for comfort. He appeared to be waiting for the lift too, but panic gripped her as they stepped into the small metal space together. She looked at the floor giving a start when he reached across her to press the button for floor nine.

'Where are you going?' he said.

'Um, seventh floor,' said Sam, which he also pressed.

The doors shut, and they journeyed up to the seventh floor.

'Do you like Kandar?' said the man.

'It's not what I expected,' said Sam.

'Have a nice time on your holiday,' he said, as she exited the lift.

Sam thanked him and walked down the passageway to the emergency stairs. Checking that the lift had gone, she pushed the door into the stairwell and descended to the sixth floor where she entered her room and shut the door, leaning on it and panting in fright. *Why didn't her credit card work? Could it be a coincidence?*

Her hands shaking, she dialled the number of the London office, listening to it ring at the other end with increasing impatience. Finally, Kelly came on the line.

'Hello, Resource Ventures. How can I help you?'

'Hi, Kelly. It's Sam.'

'Sam? Sorry I took so long to come to the phone. Leo needed tea and you know how important that is. Where are you?'

'Still in Kandar at the hotel.'

'Aren't you coming back today? We miss you, well, I do anyway.'

'I hope so. My credit card is not being accepted by the hotel system so I can't pay my bill. I'd like to get out of here for various reasons.'

'That's a bummer. What would you like me to do?' said Kelly.

'If I give you the invoice number, can you please call the hotel and pay the bill with the office credit card?' said Sam.

'Of course. Just give me a few minutes.'

'Okay, as soon as you can would be great.'

'Is everything all right over there? You sound funny,' said Kelly.

'Um, yes, fine, just busy trying to leave. I'll tell you when I get there.'

'Okay, I'll do it right now. Will you be in your room?'

'I'm going down to the reception right now. Can you text me once you've paid the bill?'

'I'll tell them to look down there for you after I've paid. Have a good trip and see you tomorrow.'

Sam descended to the reception and approached the concierge who had been observing her difficulties in paying the account with sympathy.

'Do you think you might store my bag in your cupboard until our office manager sorts out the payment of my bill, please?

'It would be my pleasure, madam. It's nice to have a polite young woman staying with us.'

Sam turned to go, but she felt uneasy about the time she had already been in the hotel.

'Um, if anyone asks for me, can you please tell them I've already left? I'm worried some people have followed me here,' she added as an afterthought.

'Naturally, madam. Why don't you wait in the café? It has a lovely view of the sea and some great pastries.'

She found a quiet corner in the café where she could see the hotel entrance through a latticework partition without being observed and she ordered a latte with only a drop of coffee in it. She sipped her coffee, heart hammering in her throat. *Could Mohammed be right about Kanté? Surely Kanté hadn't blocked her card? It must be a coincidence.*

Agitated, she picked at a scab on her arm caused by a thorn bush at Yubou. It would have been a lot deeper if the lioness had got any nearer. Suddenly, she caught sight of Amdy having an animated discussion with the concierge. He threw his arms in the air in frustration and headed for the main door. Sam jumped up and tripped over her handbag in her rush to catch up with him. Her passport and ticket shot out onto the floor.

'Amdy!' she shouted, grabbing them as fast as possible.

The concierge heard her and yelled at his departing back. Amdy stopped at the door and turned around, seeing her gesticulating at him. Behind him, a large black BMW glided up to the kerb and four men in dark suits got out and looked around outside at the tourists queuing for taxis. They surrounded a young woman with blonde hair to the chagrin of her husband.

'Run,' said Sam.

He glanced behind him at the men and walked fast through the entrance hall to where Sam stood flapping her arms in agitation. The concierge followed Amdy and pressed a door key into Sam's hand.

'Room 405,' he hissed.

Sam and Amdy ran up four flights of stairs and down the passageway to the room. Sam opened the door, and they slammed it behind them, panting.

'What the hell is going on?' said Sam. 'Who are those guys outside?'

'Kanté,' said Amdy. 'He threatened Mohammed, and he knows you have the USB stick with the Park boundary on it. He'd kill you to stop you taking it to London.'

Sam sank into one armchair and put her head in her hands. Her chest tightened around her heart. They were trapped in the hotel.

'I've got to get to the airport,' she said. 'But how do I do that without Kanté's men seeing me? There must be another route out of the hotel.'

'They won't be able to check all the rooms. There are too many, but there is only one way out of here.'

'What about a back way? Isn't there a kitchen entrance or emergency exit?'

'They'll be covering all the exits. He doesn't want you to escape.'

Sam stood up and gazed out of the window on the streets below. They were full of women in their bright-coloured dresses and headscarves carrying bundles on their heads and their backs like brightly coloured beetles scurrying along. She leaned her forehead against the glass. What a mess. She didn't even know if she could trust Amdy. *What if he'd also agreed to work with Kanté?*

She turned around. Amdy sat watching her, his almond eyes grave.

'You should've believed me,' he said.

'How did you know they'd come to get me?'

'I didn't. But when Mohammed texted me to say that Kanté was on the rampage, it became obvious I had to get you out of the hotel.'

'What are we going to do now?'

'I'm not sure. We can't stay here. Kanté will invent some pretext for having all the rooms searched.'

Sam racked her brains for a solution. How could they get past Kanté's men? She stood out like a sore thumb with her highlighted hair and western clothes. And just like that, she knew.

'Amdy, call your mother and tell her to come to our room in the hotel.'

'My mother?'

'Yes, and ask her to bring me one of her traditional outfits and your brother's walking stick. She should bring your boubou too and matching headscarves.'

'Why do you need the clothes?'

'We will walk straight past them.'

Chapter XXX

Madame Ndiaye sneaked out of the back door of her house, lugging a suitcase containing the items for which Amdy had asked her. She used her son's cane for balance and staggered across the undulating piles of waste and onto the beach where she rested, panting with exertion. She was unaccustomed to exercise as her world had shrunk over the years to her compound and the local market.

She sat on a discarded barrel and signalled to a man who was cleaning barnacles from the bottom of his skiff for assistance. He ignored her at first but came bounding over when she waved a note at him. They had an animated conversation and shook hands. Within minutes they were at sea, motoring parallel to the coast until they came to a small jetty just past the hotel.

The man helped Madam Ndiaye onto the sand and carried the suitcase onto the jetty balanced on his head. Once he had deposited it on the pavement and she had paid him for the journey, she carried the case along to the hotel entrance. Kanté's heavies did not give her a second glance as she entered the lobby and headed for the lifts simulating a limp.

Sam had become increasingly nervous as they waited for Madame Ndiaye. Time was running out if she wanted to get to the airport in time to catch her flight. She looked at her watch again and tried not to panic. Just when she was about to give up, someone knocked at the door of their room. Amdy waved her into the bathroom and went to answer it.

Amdy looked through the peephole into the hall and yelped in excitement as his mother loomed large in the passageway. He opened the door to let her enter. Beads of sweat ran down her face as he ushered her in. Sam emerged from hiding to give her a hug and helped her to a chair. While Madam Ndiaye sipped a glass of water, Amdy opened the suitcase and pulled out a bundle of clothes. He handed a wax-printed dress to Sam who took it into the bathroom to try it on. It hung loose on her body but it was close enough to her size to appear natural.

She emerged to find Amdy wearing his boubou. Madame Ndiaye beckoned her over and made her a turban which draped around her neck. Sam examined herself in the mirror and laughed. The disguise was perfect except for her face. It shone white under the fluorescent light in the bathroom.

She tipped out her handbag, searching the contents with desperation. Her hand closed on a sample tube of Egypt Wonder liquid tan given to her by Hannah for the trip. Like many of Hannah's gifts, Sam had no interest in using it but had thanked her and put it in her bag planning to eject it later. She owed Hannah a hug.

She went back into the bathroom and applied it to her face, neck and hands. When she came out again, both Amdy and his mother gasped and guffawed at the change.

'You look like a woman from Kandar now,' said Amdy.

But would her disguise get her out of the hotel?

'I'm sorry,' said Sam. 'I've got to leave or I'll miss my flight.'

'First let me take a photograph of you with my son,' said Madame Ndiaye. 'Will you send it to him?'

'Of course.'

Sam managed a smile as Amdy put his arm around her waist and posed for the shot. Sam took the camera and got a shot of Amdy and his mother together for her album of the visit. Then she put the camera back into her handbag. Would she live to send the photographs?

'Good luck, Sam,' said Madam Ndiaye. 'May Allah protect you.'

Amdy stroked her cheek. 'Goodbye, Madam,' he said.

Sam hugged them both and then slipped out of the room to the lifts with the suitcase and the cane. To her relief, she travelled down alone to the lobby. As the doors opened, she bent over simulating old age and approached the concierge's desk with a limp. He did a double-take when he recognised her but showed no sign as he removed her suitcase from his cupboard and took it to the front entrance for her.

'Good luck, Madam,' he said, winking.

She emerged out into the sunlight. Two of Kanté's men stood guard outside. One of them smoked a cigarette to one side of the entrance. Sam waved her cane at the taxi rank in front of the hotel, her heart in her throat as she prayed for one of them to notice her. The first driver, who was leaning against the door, acknowledged her signal and jumped into his car.

As his taxi approached the hotel entrance, Sam felt a light tap on her shoulder. She did not look up, grunting and hawking, and shrugging the hand off.

Black shiny shoes appeared in front of her and she readied herself for a struggle. Kanté's man reached down and picked up her suitcase. He walked around to the back of the taxi and put it into the trunk, shutting the door with a big smile.

Not believing her luck, Sam got into the back of the taxi as slowly as she could bear. She gestured a thank you with her cane at Kanté's man and said 'airport' to the driver. He pulled out slowly greeting the other taxi drivers on his way out. Sam resisted the temptation to give him the hurry up. She held her breath, but no one stopped them leaving. Relief flooded over her as she leaned back against the seat, taking a deep breath. So far so good.

The road to the airport heaved with rush hour traffic, but they made it there as the sun set over the sea. Relief flooded her body as she recognised the contours of the airport looming in the darkening African night. *What a nightmare! Henri Kanté had lived up to his reputation as a dangerous man.* She hoped Amdy had the sense to make himself scarce from now on.

The driver showed her the fare on his meter and she had a moment of fright as she remembered that she had no cash in her wallet. Just when she hyperventilated with panic, she remembered Amdy's money, stuffed into the internal pocket of her handbag. Her regret at having forgotten to give it to him, diminished with the relief at finding it. She gave the driver a decent tip and entered the check-in area.

The man at the desk took her passport and smiled at her.

'Been to a party?' he said, gesturing at her outfit.

Sam laughed. 'You could say that,' she said.

'You're cutting it fine,' he said. 'Go straight through to immigration. They'll be boarding the aircraft soon.'

Once Sam passed through security into the immigration area, she judged herself safe and entered the women's bathroom to remove her disguise, sweating from wearing it over her clothes. She folded it up and left it on a shelf, hoping it would find a good home. She washed her face and hands with the harsh soap from the bathroom sink, and removed most of the fake tan, watching it streak down into the plughole like dried blood.

She emerged from the bathroom and joined the short queue at the passport desk. The afternoon's events had taken their toll, and she longed for the cool refuge of the business class lounge. *Nearly there.* She presented her passport at the desk and waited, trying not to appear nervous. The official reviewed it at great length, glancing at her face several times. He did not give it back, but signalled to a security guard who came over to the booth.

'You must come with me, Madam,' said the guard.

'Is there a problem?' said Sam, almost fainting with fear.

'Protocol. They have flagged up your passport for some reason,' he said.

'But I'll miss my flight.'

'We'll get you to the aircraft in time. The sooner you come with me, the sooner you'll be back.'

She had no choice but to follow him back through the airport. Cold sweat dampened her shirt as she imagined a series of scenarios. *Had someone planted drugs in her suitcase?* It was in the concierge's cupboard for a long time. The guard opened a door in the corridor and gestured for her to enter.

To Sam's horror, she recognised Kanté's back facing her as she entered the bare office. He rose to meet her.

'Leaving so soon, Miss Harris? Can you please wait outside, officer?'

The guard who had accompanied Sam exited the office and shut the door, leaving them alone inside. Kanté checked the door to make sure it was closed.

'Please sit down.'

Sam dropped into the metal chair, horror gripping her. Kanté sat opposite her at the lone desk. Sam's legs were jelly.

Kanté extended his hand for her to shake. Mystified, she reciprocated. He held her hand for a moment too long, making her shudder. Kanté tensed as if ready for attack, but his words were cordial.

'So, Sam, how was your trip? My assistant tells me you collected the documents I had copied for you from my office on Friday. I hope you found everything in order.'

Sam, unsure how to take this odd conversation, replied with politeness.

'Excellent, thank you, Monsieur Kanté. The documents were the final element in my due diligence.'

Kanté raised an eyebrow.

'Indeed? So, it was a fruitful trip? Did Amdy treat you well?'

The blatant undercurrent to his question made it hard not to laugh.

'Like a queen,' she said, pretending to be embarrassed.

A lascivious expression crossed Kanté's face as he imagined the scenario.

'I'm so glad,' he said. 'We know how to treat a lady in Kandar. Speaking of which, would you like to join me for dinner tonight?'

'Next time, perhaps, I'm flying out tonight.'

'Ah, that won't be possible, I'm afraid. If you wish to leave, you must cooperate. You have something of mine. I suggest you hand it over unless you wish the situation to become unpleasant.'

He did not need to elaborate. Sam searched her handbag. Kanté put his hand out and took it from her, tipping the contents onto the desk. Among the other articles were two USB sticks. Kanté ignored them and picked up her phone. Sam froze in horror but she was powerless to stop him. He opened the photograph application and his lips formed a thin line as he examined the final photograph.

'I should've known that fool would've helped you escape. I can't believe you got by my men looking like that.'

'Oh, he didn't help me. They visited me by coincidence.'

'And who gave you the outfit? I'm not stupid, you know.'

He shoved the phone back at her and picked up the two USB sticks, one in each hand.

'Which one is it?' he said, holding them out.

'The blue one,' said Sam.

'Do you take me for a fool?' said Kanté, a shadow crossing his face.

He stood up, shoving his chair against the wall, its feet squealing on the floor.

'I want to make sure the information I need is on these. Stay here. I'm not finished with you yet.'

He swept out of the room and the guard entered and stood with his back to the door. Sam waited about thirty seconds and then refilled her handbag. She turned to face the guard.

'I have to go now or I will miss my flight,' she said.

'But I can't let you leave,' said the guard.

'I can pay you. Kanté need not know.'

Sam reached into the side pocket and took out Amdy's money. The guard's eyes widened as he took in the thick wad of cash.

'Just take me to immigration and it's all yours. Please.'

He looked around in indecision, but the temptation was too much. He opened the door and led her back through the airport almost at a run. The passport official glanced up when they arrived, but reassured by the presence of the guard, stamped her passport. She shoved the money into the guard's hand and ran. The flight would take off in half an hour and she had to make it before they shut the door, or she would use up all her cards.

She followed the signs to her gate, heart bursting with effort as she ran in and out of the dawdling passenger waiting for other flights. As she approached the gate, she could see the flight crew reaching out to close the aircraft door at the end of the passage.

'Please wait,' she shouted, sprinting now. 'Please, let me in. It's a matter of life or death.'

The steward peeped out to see who was shouting and smiled when he saw her.

'Madame Sam? Yes. You travelled out with me. I remember you. You're lucky I recognised you. Quickly or we'll miss our slot.'

Sam boarded the aircraft at a run and the door slammed shut behind her. She sank into her seat, panting, and pulled on her seat belt.

'Busy trip?' said the man sitting beside her. 'You nearly didn't make it.'

'You don't know how true that is.'

Grateful to have got out unscathed, Sam relaxed as the aircraft wheels left the ground. The view of Kandar improved as she imagined the scene when Kanté returned to the office to find her gone. He would think she had left without the information, but he would be wrong. She pulled the pouch out from where it hung between her breasts and held the warm leather, smiling with triumph. No doubt the security guard had scarpered with the money. Kanté would be incandescent with rage, but he couldn't touch her now. Edward Beckett was another matter.

Another narrow escape. After she had time to calm down, Sam reviewed the situation. Her due diligence had been a success despite the obstacles. Leo would find projects with ease now that she was notorious. Maybe working in London wasn't going to be so bad. It certainly wasn't boring.

Chapter XXXI

Edward stalked through his apartment like a tiger in a zoo, spinning on his heel as he reached the wall, and continuing his relentless pacing. He had been brooding on the deal since the call from Leo the night before. The news that Sam had obtained the data which proved the boundary of the National Park covered the exploration concession had robbed him of sleep. *Why hadn't Kanté stopped her?*

He drank another cup of coffee and tried to read the newspaper until he knew Kanté would have arrived at his office in Haribar. Then he dialled the number several times until he managed to get a ring tone.

'Henri, it's Edward. I—'

'She got away,' interrupted Kanté. 'But I took the USB stick with the evidence on it from her. She can't prove anything without it. We're running out of time to get this done. Where do we stand on the fundraising?'

'How on earth did she manage that? I thought you had it in hand.'

'I did. Somehow, she gave the guard the slip at the airport and caught her flight at the last minute. I suspect witchcraft.'

Edward ignored the reference.

'So, we can still get it done?'

'You need to get the money from the investors first. The ball's in your court now. I've done all I can. If you can't manage to raise the cash, I will be forced to raise the money elsewhere.'

'My son has it all lined up. I'll get right on it.'

'Last chance. Get the investment this week or I'll go elsewhere.'

There was no mistaking the threat in his voice. Kanté hung up. Edward sank back into the sofa and forced himself to think. His course of action became clear to him. *Leo would not allow Steven to use his clients now that he knew the project had a fatal flaw, but who needed Leo?* Now that Leo had taken Sam on, Edward wanted nothing to do with him.

The shrill buzz of the telephone echoed through the apartment, disturbing Edward's concentration on his new plan. He let it ring for a while but it kept ringing. When he picked it up, Mike Morton was in no mood for small talk.

'Edward? You took your time.'

'I'm working on something. What's the big hurry?'

'Did you sort out the access to the money yet?' said Mike.

'Not yet. These things take time. I can't just click my fingers.'

'Well, you'd better hurry up because I'm meeting Sam for a drink tomorrow and I intend to tell her about it.'

He could hear Edward breathing as he considered his options. The walls were closing in on his erstwhile partner.

'You can't. Not yet,' said Edward, who could not keep the panic out of his voice.

'Is there some problem with the money?' said Mike.

Edward sighed.

'I don't have it.'

'What do you mean, you don't have it? Surely it's in the bank?'

'Just hold off, please. It's more complicated than I thought to release the funds.'

'Okay, but I want to finish this chapter of my life and get on with the new one.'

'You couldn't want that more than me. Can you cancel the drink with Sam? I promise you'll have news soon.'

'Just get on with it.'

Mike hung up, leaving Edward shaking with anger. First the Kandar project and now this. The Harris woman had become a serious obstacle. There must be a way to persuade her to back down, but meanwhile, he had to sweet-talk Buffy Harrington.

***

Buffy Harrington waddled over to the table in the French restaurant where Edward waited, barely containing his impatience.

'Sorry, old chap, I had to make a detour to the little boy's room to point Percy at the porcelain.'

Edward's lip curled. The man was a walking cliché. If Buffy hadn't proved to be useful from time to time, he would have thrown him to the wolves years ago. He found it difficult to tolerate the stream of consciousness and weak excuses that drivelled from this lumpen, sweating, fawning individual. Buffy blundered on.

'How's the delectable Ophelia?'

Edward clenched his jaw.

'We got divorced.'

Edward's clipped tone should have warned Buffy off, but he didn't notice the frost in the air.

'Oh. Really? Never mind. Plenty more fish in the sea, what?'

Edward rolled his eyes and tapped his fingers on his side plate, his well-bitten nails clicking on the china.

'So, how's business?' said Buffy.

'Great. I have a sure-fire scheme on the boil,' said Edward.

'That's good news, excellent, but when will you able to replace the funds?'

'Soon. In the next week or so. Don't you trust me?' he said, raising his head and looking Buffy straight in the eye.

Buffy squirmed in his seat, looking left and right for a distraction. Then he held up a finger to prevent Edward from saying anything. He patted the pockets of his jacket withdrawing a copy of the Evening Standard newspaper.

'Did you see this?' he said, placing the newspaper in front of Edward and jabbing a plump finger at a photograph of Sam Harris standing between her parents. Edward raised an inquiring eyebrow, his patience with Buffy's ill-conceived attempts to avoid the subject of his massive debts. *And why was he showing him a photo of that bloody Harris woman?*

'He's my client,' said Buffy. 'Bill Harris.'

Edward's mood changed in an instant. Buffy had presented him with the perfect opportunity to kick Sam while she was down. She'd never get up again if it was anything to do with him.

'Is that so?' he said. 'Tell me about him.'
Buffy beamed.
'I gave him a loan last year to expand his business.'
Edward leaned forward.
'What's his collateral?'
Buffy blanched, fiddling with his napkin.
'Shouldn't we order?' he said.
'Don't fuck with me,' said Edwards. 'You owe me.'
'His house,' muttered Buffy.
'There. That wasn't so difficult, was it? I'll have the beef.'

Chapter XXXII

Leo put his head around the door.

'Busy?' he said.

'Never too busy for you, boss,' said Steven.

'Good, because I've some news about the Kandar project.'

Steven froze, avoiding Leo's inquiring glance.

'About the boundary?'

'Yes, Sam received the coordinates from an employee of the Directorate. The whole concession is located within the National Park.'

'What does that mean for the project?' said Steven.

'Isn't it obvious?'

Steven sank into his chair, deflated.

'Seriously? How do we know she didn't pay this guy?'

'To do what? Destroy the project? And why would she do that?'

Steven squeezed his plump fists into balls and worked himself up into a tantrum.

'How can you ask me that? She hates me, and my father. Did you know she worked for him once?' he shouted.

'I did, as a matter of fact. What makes you think she hates you, or him?'

'For a start, she tried to have me killed in Colombia. And now she's trying to discredit my father's project. Aren't you a little suspicious?'

Leo shook his head.

'And all that bullshit about being kidnapped in Tamazia. She probably lied about that too. Why was she the only survivor when they shot all the other hostages? Then her boss dies in the bath? Leo, that woman is a viper and you're being taken in. We were doing just fine until she came along, and now she's trying to destroy me.'

He was practically weeping with rage at this stage and choked to a stop.

As Leo waited for him to calm down, he spotted the notebook on Steven's desk, open at a page headed 'Kandar Fundraising'. He leaned over and to pick it up. Steven tried to grab his arm but Leo shook him free. He scanned the pages with growing alarm and wiped his brow on his sleeve to stop the sweat that had appeared from running into his eyes.

'Jesus Christ! What have you done now, you stupid little shit? Where's the money?'

'No one has paid for any shares yet, it's just a list of clients who have agreed to buy the offering.'

'And the numbers?'

'Their expected buy-in. Listen, Leo, you must believe me. Sam is not the angel she makes herself out to be. You are being taken for an idiot. Mark my words.'

'It's not me who's the idiot,' said Leo.

He stomped back to his office and slammed the door. He had had just about enough of Steven Horgan. Once Sam got back, he would go out on his own with her. He started leafing through the reports on his desk trying to find a good one among the chaff, but no matter how many times he read them, even he couldn't find a reason to invest in any of them.

The phone rang. Edward's number showed on the display. Leo took a deep breath.

'Good morning,' he said. 'What's up?'

'Steven just told me about Sam,' said Edward. 'I've had enough of that woman interfering in my projects.'

'Interfering? She's doing her job. The project is a dud.'

'Only according to her. Anyway, I've decided to raise the funds without you. Steven will work with me now.'

'What about the clients?'

'Oh, I'm taking them with me.'

Leo could hear him smiling. He took a deep breath.

'And the office?'

'You can have a month but after that it's mine.'

'Jesus, Edward, you'll bankrupt me. This is not what we agreed.'

'Six weeks for old time's sake. Then I want you out.'

The phone line went dead and a dial tone buzzed in Leo's ear. He sat there listening to its shrill sound until Kelly appeared at his door with a cup of coffee.

'What's wrong, Leo? You look like you've seen a ghost,' she said.

'We're in trouble,' said Leo. 'Edward is pulling down the shutters in six weeks' time.'

Kelly gasped.

'What are we going to do?' she said.

At that moment, Sam arrived from the airport, entering the office beaming with triumph.

'I'm back,' she said to resounding silence.

Kelly turned tear-filled eyes to her, trying to smile. Leo gave her a shrug.

'Good to see you,' he said. 'I've got some news. You'd better come in.'

Feeling a bit underwhelmed by her welcome, Sam followed him in.

'Is it the project?' said Sam. 'I've got proof that it's a scam right here on a USB stick.'

'It's project related. You did amazing work out there at no little risk to your own safety, but it also convinced Edward to keep the project for himself and to use Steven to sell it.'

Sam tried not to appear pleased. It seemed like the perfect result.

'So, what are we going to do?' she said. 'Have you got something else for me to review? We can go it alone.'

'Edward's taking the office back. If we don't find somewhere else to go, it will finish us,' said Leo.

'But there must be another office we can rent,' said Sam.

'Yes, but we need money for the deposit and furnishings. We must do a deal before the deadline or it's curtains for Resource Ventures.'

'Do we still have clients?'

'Edward is taking his with him, but I have some decent investors left. The problem is that I can't afford to pay you after the end of this month as it stands.'

'Oh.'

Sam had trouble keeping the tears in. She had risked her life to prove Edward's project a dud, but it had backfired. Life had bitten back.

'I'm rather tired,' she said. 'I didn't sleep on the flight back so I'm going home. Can we talk about this later?'

'I'm sorry you came home to this news after all your efforts. Let me think about it. Maybe I can come up with a solution.'

Chapter XXXIII

Her parents were at a loss to deal with Sam's sense of shock and betrayal when she came home early from work and declared she would lose her job. Unusually for her, she wept copiously, unable to control the waves of resentment and feelings of injustice racking her. She had done her job well, but that had got her fired and lost Leo the office. Somehow her good work had produced a disaster again.

The worst thing about it was Steven's reaction. He leaned into her office, cock-a-hoop with the news and gave her a two-fingered salute.

'It's about time you got your comeuppance, you bitch. A loser like you would never defeat my father. Good luck finding another job after he talks to his friends about you. You're toast, Sam Harris. Go back to the jungle where you belong.'

Before she could dredge up a retort, he had gone, grabbing Kelly's bottom on the way out, making her hiss with fury. Sam had left the office soon after, unable to bear the atmosphere.

When Sam had calmed down a little, her mother made the obligatory cup of tea and shoved a tentative slice of fruit cake at her. Sam picked at it without enthusiasm.

'There's no need to sulk, darling. You did your best. Can't you find another job?' said Matilda Harris. 'Now that you're famous and everything.'

'I don't want another job,' said Sam. 'Edward is closing the office because of me. I won't give up. I owe Leo that. One of my old contacts will have a project. I'm going to call them all and dig up one for us. One good deal will save us.'

'That's the spirit,' her father said.

Sam sighed. If only it were so easy.

For the next few days, Sam sat at her computer in the office sending emails to her contacts all over the world. She looked up junior companies on the London and Toronto stock exchanges and contacted them asking if they were looking for finance for advanced exploration projects. She even rang her friends in Sierramar and asked them to spread the word. Gloria had squealed with excitement at Sam's call.

'Are you coming home soon?' said Gloria. 'We all miss you. Even Yannis has been calling.'

'Yannis?'

The heat rose in her face as she remembered her time with him on the beach in Esmeraldas.

'He's missing you. You should come and see us. Who cares about your stupid job? They don't appreciate you like we do,' said Gloria.

'I promise to come and visit after Christmas, but you need to help me. I owe Leo a good project. Can you visit the Chamber of Mines and put the word about please?'

'Okay, but you have to come soon. You haven't even met Mia yet.'

'I'll come once I get this sorted out. Look after Alfredo and the babies.'

Gloria grunted and whispered goodbye close to tears.

A visit to Sierramar, especially one that involved a sojourn with Yannis, buoyed Sam's mood and she redoubled her efforts to find a project for Leo. Requests for funding flooded in from all over the globe. *Why hadn't she done this before?'*

Swamped by possibilities, Sam stayed late at the office reviewing pages and pages of exploration reports. She received a few projects that had good prospects but nothing which had any drilling, a prerequisite for their funding. Leo shook his head at her enthusiasm.

'You never give up, do you?'

'Never. I'll find you a project if it kills me.'

'This isn't your fault, Sam.'

'No, but it sure feels like it. Let me do this.'

Sam's parents had called a family conference at the Harris household. These only occurred once in a blue moon and the Harris sisters were mystified as to the subject. Hannah arrived on time for once and Sam opened the front door for her. The two women headed into the sitting room, the traditional setting for these family meetings.

Sam dropped onto the sofa with a satisfied sigh as she eyed the tray balanced on the footstool in front of her. Her list of projects had lengthened, and she was close to finding the perfect candidate. She reached out to select a chocolate biscuit and a mug of tea. Beside her, Hannah filed an already perfect nail and picked at a ragged cuticle, her face a picture of disgust at the rogue piece of skin.

Their parents came in holding hands, which struck Sam as odd. She couldn't remember ever seeing them do that before. A cold chill hit her stomach. This could not be good news. The Harris parents separated and sat opposite each other in the armchairs matching the sofa occupied by their daughters. Bill Harris cleared his throat. Sam looked up from her plate where she had been harvesting the crumbs to calm her nerves.

'What's the big announcement?' said Hannah, who hadn't picked up on the strained air in the room. 'Are you pregnant?'

Matilda Harris made a sound which resembled a sob, stifled with her napkin before it could escape.

'Mummy? What's wrong?' said Sam, looking from one to another.

'We're in trouble,' said Bill Harris. 'I got a loan from the bank to put into my business last year and the manager called me this week to call it in.'

'Can they do that? Don't you have to miss payments or something?' said Sam.

'I was late on a couple of payments, but that was months ago, and I informed the bank that they would be late because of temporary cash flow problems. I don't understand why Buffy has changed his mind, but there's nothing I can do.'

'Buffy? What sort of name is that?' said Sam.

'Buffy Harrington. He's old school. He comes from a long line of Buffies and Bunnies and Porkies,' said Bill.

Sam snorted.

'Don't be silly, dear,' said Matilda. 'This is serious.'

'Why didn't you tell us?' said Hannah.

'We didn't want to worry you,' her mother said.

'And we were sure we could change his mind, but it has proved impossible. It makes little sense. Perhaps he has some sort of quotas to fill.'

'What happens next?' said Sam.

'The bank has given us three months to raise the cash or they will foreclose and sell the house. If that happens, we must move out,' said Bill.

'Why did you invest so much in the business?' said Hannah. 'Wasn't it already making a profit?'

'We were hoping to make enough to give you both a deposit for houses of your own.'

A wave of shame swamped Sam, making it hard to breathe. The biscuit sat in her stomach like a lead brick.

'I've been complaining about losing my job, but you haven't told me anything about this. It's awful,' she said.

'I tried to get a new loan,' her father said. 'I didn't want to worry you.'

'When will you know?' said Hannah.

'Soon, darling,' her mother said, a tear running down her cheek making a trail in the face powder she used.

Silence reigned while the family members controlled their feelings and searched for something neutral to say.

'But where will you go?' said Hannah.

'Oh, don't worry about us. We'll think of something,' said Bill. 'We still have three months to sort this out.'

Sam returned to the office on Monday with a black cloud hanging over her. Not even a stream of emails filled with news of projects looking for a backer could cheer her up. She hadn't told Kelly about Kandar yet.

The whole thing seemed preposterous to her now, as if she had imagined it.

Another story she wouldn't tell but would lock up in her memory instead of blurting it out on her rare nights out with friends, where she got the distinct impression that she was breaking some unwritten code about showing off. Thus, the memories piled up over the years, running around her head like a herd of bison stampeding in a corral with no gate.

She looked up at the skylight where the weak London sunshine was filtering through onto the board table, barely creating a shadow. Quite a contrast to Kandar. She had her fingers crossed that Amdy would save enough to buy a second-hand motorbike and ride to another town for work. If he disappeared, his brother would have to get off his fat behind and make an effort. And as for Kanté, she had had a lucky escape there. The man radiated evil.

Sam sighed and reviewed the new emails in her inbox. To her surprise, she had received an email with an attachment from Mohammed. Perhaps there would be news of Amdy. She clicked on the email, scanning it and then she stopped, horrified. She stared at her screen, trying to focus her brain. The words swam before her eyes. Amdy est mort. Appelle-moi s'il vous plait. *Dead? How could he be dead?*

She pulled the telephone towards her with shaking hands and dialled Mohammed's number. The line dropped several times before she could hear the ring tone.

'Hello?'

'Mohammed, this is Sam, your cousin's friend. You sent me an email.'

'Sam? I'm so glad you rang. Are you alone?'

'Alone? Yes. Why?'

'Because this is confidential. I don't know who might be involved.'

'I can't believe Amdy is dead,' said Sam 'You have my sincere condolences.'

'Thank you. We're all in a state of shock here.'

'What happened to him?'

'The official version is that he fell over a cliff. But no one accepts that.'

Sam gasped.

'I'm so sorry,' she said. 'I should never have got him involved with all of this. He's dead because of me. How did he die?'

'Rumour has it that someone hit him with a tyre iron, and then threw his body over the cliff,' said Mohammed.

'He was murdered? But how do you know?'

'His mother told me he got a phone call from Kanté in the middle of the night, sending him to collect a man from Faro, the town to the east of Haribar. Kanté offered Amdy lots of money. Amdy set off to collect the client, and he never returned.'

'So, what makes you think they murdered him? Maybe he had an accident?'

'The cliff is in the middle of nowhere, to the north of Haribar. It isn't on the route to Faro.'

'But who would have done this?' said Sam, even though she knew.

'There is a rumour going around that Grand Derrière put out a contract. He's a dangerous man to cross. What did you two do to him?'

Sam remembered the photo. Surely they didn't kill him over that? But her report destroyed his project. He must have been furious. Maybe he killed Amdy for revenge?

'We hit him where it hurts. In the wallet. What do the police say? Can they pin it on him?'

A dry laugh crackled over the line.

'Sam, you are so European. Do you imagine the police can touch him?'

'I'm so sorry. I feel responsible.'

'That trip with you was the best thing that ever happened to him, Sam. He lived like a free man for the first time in his life. He told me you saved his life. You should be proud. Be careful, I don't know if Grand Derrière has friends in London, but I would watch my back if I were you.'

The line went dead. Sam sat alone for a minute before clicking on the attachment. It was a photograph of Amdy, El Hadji and Sam in the restaurant in Haribar. It made her smile despite her sadness. She stood up and approached Kelly's desk.

'Do you want to have lunch?' she said. 'I've had some news and I need a shoulder.'

Chapter XXXIV

Mike had commandeered the snug in the corner of the Bull and Bear and sat at a small round table smoking a cigar with concentrated pleasure. He tapped the ash off into an ashtray bearing the pub's crest and took a long draft of his pint of lager, leaving a trail of foam on his upper lip. He licked it off and wiped his chin on a napkin as a drop of lager left a chilly trail on it.

Edward entered the pub by the lounge door and having searched the area came through into the bar, spotting Mike ensconced in the corner. He wrinkled his nose at the smell of Mike's cigar.

'Can't you put out that abomination? It stinks,' he said.

'And hello to you too. What's up now? Princess Anne could take lessons in disgusted from you.'

'Hilarious. I happen to admire her. She's a hardworking member of the Royal family unlike some others I could mention.'

'Imitation is the sincerest form of flattery,' said Mike, swigging down the last of his pint. 'What can I get you?'

'I'll have a gin and tonic, please. Make it a double.'

Mike couldn't help smiling. Edward always had a double since Mike had hit it big, as if he was trying to recoup his investment in the lean years. He ordered another lager with the gin and tonic, and some cheese and onion crisps, mostly because it would annoy Edward.

'Here we go old son, get that inside you and tell Uncle Mike all your woes.'

'Cut the crap. This is important.'

Mike slid into the faux velvet bench facing Edward and put the drinks down on the table, slopping some lager onto the varnished top. Edward sighed as Mike tried to mop it up with some already soggy napkins. Mike ignored him and opened the crisps, offering them to Edward who recoiled in horror.

'I'm listening,' said Mike.

'I won't pay Sam that money,' said Edward. 'The woman's a charlatan. She tried to swindle me.'

Mike snorted into his lager.

'Sam? You're having a laugh. Little miss goody-two-shoes tried to swindle you? Never. I don't believe it.'

His laughter rebounded around the walls of the snug making people lift their heads from their newspapers and drinks to see what the commotion was about. Edward sneered.

'Well, miss butter-wouldn't-melt-in-her-mouth just got herself fired for trying to get my project cancelled.'

Mike's lager hovered in the air below his mouth as he scrutinised Edward for signs he had indulged in irony or hyperbole. He raised an eyebrow.

'Fired? Are you sure?'

'Of course. I made damn sure.'

'Did you now?' said Mike, his bonhomie evaporating. 'So, now you don't want to pay her the money we owe either? Is that right?'

'You've got it in one.'

Mike looked Edward in the eye.

'Well, you can fuck right off, you bastard. I'd no more believe that of Sam than I would of the Virgin Mary. You've got an agenda, mate. So, don't come in here all hoity-toity and expect me to kowtow to your little schemes. Sam is entitled to that money and I'll give it to her whether you like it or not. You can't stop me.'

Edward digested this tirade.

'I wouldn't bet on it,' he said. He stood up and left Mike gasping with indignation, the crisps spilling out of his hand into the pool of beer on the table.

Sam and Kelly were having a chat at Kelly's desk when the telephone rang. Kelly grabbed it and put on her official greeting voice.

'Hello, Resource Ventures. Yes, she's here.'

Kelly put her hand over the receiver.

'It's Mike Morton for you,' she said, raising her eyebrows.

Sam put out her hand to take the telephone, wagging her finger at Kelly in denial.

'Mike? Yes, you just caught me.'

She nodded. 'Now? Okay, I'll meet you there. See you soon.'

She handed the receiver back to Kelly.

'Got a date?' said Kelly.

'I have,' said Sam. 'I'm meeting Mike Morton for a drink in the Clarence.'

Leo, who had been earwigging stepped out of his office, his eyes wide.

'Mike Morton? How do you know him?' he said.

Sam laughed.

'We have a past,' she said. 'I'll tell you about it sometime.'

Judging by his amazed expression, Leo had picked up the wrong end of the stick but Sam didn't have time to disabuse him. She winked at Kelly and, grabbing her coat and handbag, swept out of the office.

Leo came to stand beside Kelly's desk. He rubbed his chin and snorted.

'Well, that's a turnabout for the books. Sam and Mike Morton? I'd never have guessed. She sure is a dark horse.'

Still shaking his head, he turned on his heel and went back into his office, shutting the door behind him.

Sam found Mike sitting at the back of the Clarence pub, a big grin on his face. He looked worse than he had in the discotheque. His bald head shone under the spotlighting and his bright blue eyes examined her as she approached.

'Hello,' he said. 'Long time no see.'

Grey-faced, he sank back into his seat, wheezing like an old man.

'Are you okay?' said Sam. 'Your lungs sound like ancient bellows.'

'Oh, it's nothing. Just getting a cold.'

'It doesn't sound like a cold.'

'Old age,' said Mike.

'You're hardly old,' said Sam. 'You look worse than I feel.'

'That would be difficult,' said Mike. 'I'm so sorry about your job. Edward can be a bastard when he doesn't get what he wants.'

'I can cope with losing my job, but now it seems I'm losing my home too. The bank is foreclosing on my father's loan. We'll all be out on the street because of some clown called Buffy.' Sam didn't notice the surprise on Mike's face. 'Who calls their son Buffy? It's like a joke.'

Mike took a gulp of his beer.

'Buffy Harrington? Oh my God, it's worse than I thought. Edward has never been a nice man, but I never figured him for a criminal. He must be desperate.'

'A criminal' said Sam. 'What do you mean?'

'Buffy Harrington is under Edward's thumb for some reason I've never understood. This has Edward's hallmark all over it. How on earth did he find out that your father had a loan at Buffy's bank?'

Sam had gone white with shock.

'I've lost my job and my parents are losing their home because of me,' she said. 'I should never have come to work in London. It's been a disaster from start to finish.'

'Not all of it. Your reputation has been enhanced by your ability to spot a scam,' said Mike. He laughed at her glum expression. 'That's not necessarily a good thing with all the shady deals going on in the mining business.'

'Too honest to employ, you mean?' said Sam. 'I think you may be right.'

'There's something else I haven't told you,' said Mike.

***

The journey home took forever. An unplanned tube strike had forced the cancellation of most of the trains, and the buses were on go-slow in sympathy. Sam sat upstairs in a Routemaster fighting the urge to get out and run, knowing it was too far. Finally, she couldn't bear it and she took to the streets, weaving in and out of the Christmas crowds on Oxford street until she got to Marble Arch where she jumped in a taxi.

'14 Acacia Avenue, please. As quick as you can.'

'There's a speed limit, love,' said the driver, but seeing her distraught face in the mirror, he put his foot down, anyway.

Even with the driver's best efforts, the journey seemed to take forever. When they arrived at the Harris house, Sam thrust a note into his hand.

'Keep the change.'

'Happy Christmas, love. Hope it turns out to be a good one.'

Sam burst into the door of her parent's house surprising Bill and Matilda who were watching an episode of Rosemary and Thyme.

'Hello, darling,' her father said. 'Your mother's making notes on new ways to murder me. Did you have a nice evening?'

'I've been with Mike Morton,' said Sam.

Her parents turned in unison to stare at her, programme forgotten.

'This calls for a cup of tea,' her father said.

'What about your series?' said Sam.

'They'll repeat it ad nauseam,' her mother said.

Sam flashed her father an astonished expression. They all filed into the kitchen and soon a massive pot of tea brewed on the table.

'Mike Morton? Now there's a blast from the past,' said Bill Harris. 'What did the reprobate have to say for himself? Didn't he make a fortune in the dot-com boom?'

'I can't think of anyone who deserves it less,' said Matilda.

'Don't be mean-spirited,' said Sam. 'Bygones are bygones. Anyway, he had important news for me. He used Sierramar Holdings as the shell company for his pet food company.'

'Isn't that the company you had shares in?' her father said.

Sam beamed.

'I still have,' she said. 'Well, not shares, Mike sold them all.'

Her mother tutted.

'Honestly, darling. Will you never learn? That man is a charlatan.'

'I like him,' said Sam. 'He's so transparent. I'm well aware of his failings and what to expect from him. Anyway, as I was saying, Mike sold my shares and put the money in trust for me at Barclays.'

Her mother put her cup down on the table with a thud, making them all jump.

'How much money?'

'I'm not sure, he couldn't remember, a lot of money. I have to speak to the manager to organise a transfer. Mike says he's given his permission for me to remove the money from the account.'

'It sounds amazing, but I advise caution,' said Bill. 'A leopard doesn't change his spots. What was the name of his company again?'

'Food 4 Pets,' said Sam. 'He set it up by mortgaging his house.'

'Did he tell his wife?' said Matilda.

'He didn't say,' said Sam.

'I bet he didn't,' said Bill. 'Anyway, he sold it for many millions, so I don't expect she cares now. Your share must be considerable,' he said.

'It is,' said Sam. 'I don't want to jinx it by telling you, but I think I might be able to buy a small flat.'

'Congratulations, darling. No one deserves it more than you.'

'Don't congratulate me yet. Mike hasn't changed. It could evaporate,' said Sam.

'Why don't you know any normal people?' said Matilda.

'I know you, mummy,' said Sam.

Chapter XXXV

'Hello, Buffy Harrington here. Who's speaking?'

Edward's oily tones invaded his ear.

'Buffy old chap, I need a favour.'

Another favour. Buffy winced at the thought.

'Of course, Eddy, what can I do for you?'

An intake of breath. Edward hated diminutives.

'We've got a problem. Do you remember showing me the photo of Sam Harris and her father?'

'Naturally. I foreclosed his mortgage as instructed. The poor man is about to lose his house. Was that necessary?'

'The foreclosure didn't work. This woman is like an invasion of bedbugs. It's no good killing a few, you have to burn the mattress too.'

Buffy did not like the simile.

'I'm not doing anything violent. I can't stand the sight of blood.'

Edward laughed.

'Don't be idiotic. I'm not asking you to do that.'

'Well, what is it then? Because I've had enough of doing you favours. This is the last one. Next time I'll go to the police and hand myself in rather than be beholden to you all my life.'

'Calm down. It's only a small task. Mike Morton told her about the money we put in trust for her in Barclays, and she's coming to see you to get the money transferred. I want you to tell her she can't have the cash without the original share certificate. Can you do that for me?'

Buffy tried to think of a reason not, but his fear of Edward got the better of him.

'Okay, but I'm telling you, this is the last time. No more favours.'

Buffy didn't have to wait long for Sam to make an appointment. He didn't even bother to fob her off, which amazed her. She turned up at the bank early but was shown straight to his office. His scrutiny of her made her feel uncomfortable.

'Miss, um, ah, Harris isn't it?'

'Yes, that's me,' said Sam.

'You've come about the trust?'

'Yes, Mike Morton told me to see you.'

'Have you got the certificate?'

'What certificate?'

'The share certificate. I need to verify authenticity before I do the transfer.'

Buffy folded his arms and glared at her as is daring her to dispute his claim. Sam couldn't believe that she'd heard correctly.

'The share certificates? But that was nearly fifteen years ago. I'm not sure I have one any more.'

'I'm sorry, but it says right here that you must bring the original certificate to claim the money.'

Buffy poked at a document with his fat index finger but he didn't offer to let Sam read what they wrote there. She didn't call his bluff. The certificate had been in a drawer in the kitchen ever since she had received it. She took it out with great ceremony now and then when entertaining fantasies of being rich. Her parents never cleaned out the drawers. It would still be there.

'I have the document at home. Do you need me to bring anything else with me?'

Buffy coloured and stuttered.

'Um, no, at least, I don't think so.'

He radiated uncertainty. Sam wondered if her answer had been unexpected. Edward would hover in the background on this one. He would never let her get the money if he could stop her somehow, but his options were running out and Mike had signed the letter. She shook his hand.

'I'll be back,' she said.

***

But the certificate had disappeared.

'The weirdest thing has happened. I've ransacked the whole house but I can't find the certificate anywhere. I don't understand,' said Matilda Harris, shrugging as she folded the tea towels she had picked up from the table, and replaced them in the drawer.

'Maybe it's fallen down behind a cupboard?' said Sam.

'Your father moved everything about but the certificate has vanished. I'm sorry, sweetheart. I know you didn't need this news after all you've been through, but I fear it may be gone forever,' her mother said.

'But I can't get the money without the certificate,' said Sam, feeling sick.

'I'm sure it will turn up. I have thrown nothing out.'

Sam looked around at the furniture marks on the floor and the piles of scattered paper on the kitchen table. Her father's organised folder of guarantees and instructions for the electrical equipment was strewn across the counter. She shook her head and collected them into a pile.

'This chaos is not all bad,' her mother said. 'I was planning on going through the lot before our move, anyway. I need to throw away all the redundant instructions and vitamin brochures.'

Sam felt a wave of sympathy for her mother, a woman who would find the positive in a nuclear explosion. She wanted to hug her, but Matilda Harris was not a hugger. Instead, she put on the kettle and warmed the teapot with some boiling water. A cup of tea was the surest sign of love and support in the Harris household, and never open to misinterpretation.

'Thank you, darling,' her mother said.

Later in the day, Sam hung her head and wept on the front step of her parent's house. Her last chance had evaporated. Her career as an analyst had come to a premature end after the debacle with the Kandar Project. None of this was her fault, but no one cared. They had moved on to the next big thing. She would have to go back to the jungle again just when she had adjusted to being at home. And that home would not exist next time she got back on leave. Edward Beckett had seen to that.

She stood up, wiping her eyes on her sleeve and entered the front hall imagining the echo as her feet trod on bare floorboards. She pictured the empty rooms, the shadows of paintings removed from walls, the miscellaneous paper clips and elastic bands scattered on the floor and stuck in the gaps between the floorboards. What a disaster. She began to cry again, the sobs racking her chest and crackling in her lungs. An arm snaked around her shoulders.

'So that's where you are. Don't cry, sis. We'll get through this.'

Sam turned to Hannah, tears staining her T-shirt.

'This is all my fault. I might have prevented the sale of the house.'

'Don't be silly. How could this be your fault? It's just life.'

'No, the certificate, I could have—'

Hannah put her hands onto Sam's shoulders and held her at arm's length, her face serious for once.

'The what?'

'Share certificate,' said Sam. 'I've lost it. The proceeds would have saved the house.'

Hannah gasped and her hand flew to her mouth. Then she gurgled as a laugh escaped from her throat. An astonished Sam stared at her as if she were mad.

'What is wrong with you? This isn't funny, it's terrible.'

'No, it's funny. Really.'

'I don't understand.'

'You mean the certificate that has lived in the kitchen drawer for the past umpteen years?'

Sam nodded.

'I have the certificate,' said Hannah, giggling.

Sam choked.

'Why? What on earth have you done with it?'

'I left the old thing at the art framing shop. I thought you'd like to put the framed certificate on your wall as a reminder of the good old days. I planned to give it to you for Christmas.'

Sam stared at her and mouthed words that wouldn't come out.

'We can collect the document now. My car's outside,' said Hannah. 'What do you need it for, anyway?'

Sam ran to where her parents were sitting on a bench in the park opposite the house. They held hands and stared at the ducks on the lake. She planted herself in front of them, face still shiny with tears.

'You will never guess what just happened.'

***

Buffy examined the certificate and compared the name to the one on her passport. A rivulet of sweat crept down the side of his face. He did not look Sam in the face, sighing loudly several times as if in a discussion with himself. Finally, he stood up and went over to the door. He checked outside as if he imagined someone would eavesdrop on them.

'The money's gone,' he said. 'I'm so sorry.'

'Gone, how could it be gone?' said Sam.

'Edward Beckett,' said Buffy, wiping his brow with an ancient handkerchief. 'I tried to stop him but he took it.'

'But you work for the bank,' said Sam. 'I don't understand.'

'He knows things,' said Buffy. 'Things about me.'

He almost wept with shame. Starting to appreciate just who she was dealing with, an annoying wave of sympathy hit Sam as she watched him flap helpless hands and mop rivers of sweat from his fat face.

'And my father's mortgage?' said Sam, driving the knife deeper.

'I had no choice,' said Buffy. 'You don't know what he's like.'

'I'll go to the police,' said Sam, knowing she wouldn't.

'Please don't. I have a family.' He blew his nose. 'What if I restore your father's loan? Edward's the one you want, not me.'

'You can do that?' said Sam.

'Restoration will take me a couple of days, but there is a precedent for this. I'm sick of Edward bullying me. I have to fight back. You should do something about that man. He'll get away with murder one of these days.'

'But he's got contacts everywhere. How do we find the information to do that?'

'Behind every powerful man is a woman,' said Buffy, a shy smile creeping onto his face. 'You need to speak to Ophelia. Cherchez la femme.'

Chapter XXXVI

Ophelia Beckett took a sip from her Sauvignon Blanc mirroring Sue Ellen Ewing on the television. Drinking along with repeats of Dallas was still one of her favourite games, one she indulged in downstairs now that she had banished Edward, and more often since her friends had had enough of her divorce drama and moved on.

Despite her original triumph, after being awarded many of Edward's possessions in the divorce, she still felt cheated. She had struggled to fill the days, rattling around their house in Regent's Park like a lone penny in a collection box. When the invitations to join their friends at social events dried up, she came to the slow realisation that Edward held all the cards in that arena.

The doorbell rang, making her jump with its shrill insistence. She hauled herself off the couch with a sigh and shuffled to the front door which she threw open with a little more panache than she had intended. Her false eyebrows struggled to rise on her Botox-ravaged face as she registered the presence of Mike and Sam on her doorstep. She looked from one to the other in disbelief, focusing on Sam.

She cocked her head to one side and her eyes swivelled left as she searched her memory bank. A smile ghosted across her face.

'Pam, isn't it? We met in Lindos all those years ago.'

'Um, it's Sam, Sam Harris. Yes, we did.'

Ophelia turned to Mike.

'You've got a cheek turning up here when this is all your fault,' she said, poking him in the chest with a bony finger. But there was no aggression in her gesture, just a gentle sadness.

'You'd better come in, I suppose.'

The house looked the same as it had when Edward lived there except for a few, plump, Habitat scatter-cushions balanced on the leather sofa looking out of place in the cosy Edwardian decor. The sitting room smelt of clandestine cigarettes despite the bowls of potpourri and a stick of incense burning on the coffee table. Ophelia draped herself along the couch, leaning her head on her hand and inviting comment.

'You look good,' Mike forced out. 'Single life suits you.'

To Sam's jaundiced eye, Ophelia looked like roadkill which had lost its meat and she struggled not to say so. A more blatant rebellion lurked in the form of a Siamese cat stalking flies among the thick velvet drapes on the sash windows. Ophelia smirked when she spotted Mike's face as the cat ran its claws down the heavy velvet.

'My little present to myself,' she said. 'Edward hates cats. Sit down and tell me what I can do for such an odd couple. I presume it's Edward related?'

She took a swig from her wine glass, leaving another smear of lipstick on its already murky exterior, surveying them to see who would speak first.

Mike broke before Sam under her icy glare.

'We need your help...' He petered off, waving his hands in the air under her amused stare.

'What's he done now?' she said.

'He's selling a useless mining project to investors, and he's stolen my money,' said Sam.

Ophelia scarcely blinked.

'Honestly, if you think that's bad, you haven't met my husband. I've got files upstairs that would make you faint.'

Mike leaned forward and refilled her glass.

'What files?' he said.

'Oh, you remember, those projects he worked on with you over the years. Some of them were not kosher.'

Mike blushed.

'And you of all people should know,' she added.

'So, will you help us?' said Sam. 'There isn't any hope of his City friends helping us. See no evil, hear no evil, speak no evil, if you understand what I mean.'

Ophelia pouted.

'It's all very well coming here to Aunt Ophelia and asking for sweeties but what have you got to give me in return? This information is priceless and there are many who would pay a lot to have it. Edward is not exactly flavour of the month in some circles. It's not only you who is looking for revenge.'

She lay back on the sofa humming and ignoring them.

'Come on, old girl. You want to get him back as much as we do. Give us a break,' said Mike.

'Forget it. And as for calling me old girl, you're not doing yourself any favours here, Morton.'

'I've got money,' said Mike.

'I don't need your money,' said Ophelia.

Mike shrugged and turned to Sam. As he watched, her eyes lit up, and she bit her lip.

'Um, were you aware Edward owned an office in Mayfair?'

Ophelia's eyes opened wide. She swung her legs off the sofa and put down her wine glass, suddenly sober.

'Tell me more,' she hissed, reminding Sam of Cruella De Vil more every minute.

'I work for a guy called Leo Giustra who runs a broking business called Resource Ventures from an attic in Dover Street. He told me it belonged to Edward,' said Sam.

'The business?' said Ophelia, slurring slightly.

'The office,' said Sam. 'By my reckoning, at least half of it is yours.'

Ophelia clapped her hands together in delight.

'You clever girl. I knew he had hidden things from me, I just couldn't trace them.'

'I think Leo knows the name of the offshore company that holds the office if that helps,' said Sam. 'I could ask him for you.'

Ophelia leapt to her feet and danced about, shouting yes, yes, yes.

'It wouldn't surprise me if he had other properties hidden in there,' said Mike, feeding her frenzy.

'Other properties? It all makes sense to me now. You've hit the jackpot, Sam.'

'So, can you help us?' said Sam.

'I've got enough to put the man in prison for the rest of his life.'

Sam joined Ophelia in her dance, watched by a bemused Mike, who didn't seem so excited by this news. He cleared his throat stopping them in their tracks.

'I hate to burst your bubble, Ophelia, but since you were aware of this malfeasance, you might also go to prison. We'll need to review the projects and select the ones in which neither you nor I were involved.'

'So how will we get the information to the police?' said Sam.

'We have to be careful. Edward is a freemason,' said Ophelia.

'That's not great news,' said Mike. 'Most of the senior officers in the Met are also members. They stick together like glue.'

'How about a leak to the press?' said Ophelia.

'Edward is friends with most of the press barons,' said Mike. 'I'm not sure anyone would be brave enough to publish.'

'I know someone,' said Sam.

Chapter XXXVII

For the next few days, Mike and Sam searched through the treasure trove unearthed by Ophelia. She became animated and hyperactive as she enjoyed the company of her co-conspirators, disappearing into the kitchen to urge her cook to produce mammoth meals of delicious food to keep them going.

'You are worse than my mother,' said Sam, gorging on a steak and kidney pie with Guinness-based gravy. 'I'm putting on weight just by looking at this food.'

'Don't forget to leave room for dessert. Cook has made us a blackberry and apple crumble.'

Mike groaned. 'I need new trousers.'

By the end of the week, they had separated three files from the rest. After Leo had given the name of the offshore company used to buy the office in Mayfair to Sam, it had been easy to dig up the other illegal schemes run out of it. Edward had avoided a huge tax bill, swindled an investor out of two million pounds and bought the office in Mayfair all under the same umbrella.

Ophelia served them all a gin and tonic and they sat on the sofas in the downstairs sitting room. Sam burped loudly, making Mike giggle.

'We have our projects,' said Ophelia. 'How do we get this stuff published?'

'Didn't you say that you knew someone Sam?' said Mike.

'I did,' said Sam, hesitating. 'It's just that—'

'Oh, for God's sake,' broke in Ophelia. 'Don't tell me you're emotionally entangled with this journalist. That's all we need.'

'Not any more,' said Sam. 'I just haven't seen him since the break-up.'

'Are you sure you're okay with this?' said Mike. 'We can check if someone on the Standard will break the curfew.'

'Absolutely,' said Sam. 'I have to speak to him sometime. No time like the present.'

Ophelia tutted.

'Be like me. Take everything and run.'

'I'll keep that in mind,' said Sam.

She made Mike and Ophelia sit in the kitchen while she rang Fergus from the sitting room. Despite this, Sam was sure she could hear drunken giggling in the hall outside. She rolled her eyes to heaven and waited for him to pick up.

'Hello, Fergus Dockrell here.'

'Um, hi. It's—'

'Sam? I thought I'd lost you. Where did you disappear to? I felt terrible after our meeting. I didn't have time to explain, you know, about Aimee.'

'Aimee? God no, I'm not calling about that. This is business. Can you meet me to talk about a scoop?'

Fergus's throaty laugh echoed down the line.

'A scoop? Seriously?'

'Why is that so funny? Don't you think I could generate one?'

'You mean this isn't an excuse to see me?'

'No, it isn't. Are you interested or not?

'Naturally. Can you come to the office after work? Say, seven o'clock?'

At seven sharp Sam entered the lobby of the building where Fergus had his office. She travelled up in the lift, checking her lipstick in the shiny chrome surface and trying to stay calm. She adjusted the files under her arm as the lift doors opened and walked down the corridor, her knees knocking.

Fergus stood at the door waiting for her. She stopped in front of him, uncertain how to greet him. He lurched forward to kiss her cheek as she stuck out her hand and there was a tangle of limbs as they bumped together in confusion.

'Well, that was awkward,' said Fergus. 'I'm so sorry, Sam. I—'

'No, I'm the one who is sorry. I shouldn't have sprung the whole relationship thing on you. I didn't realise you were already spoken for,' said Sam. 'Anyway, that's not why I'm here.'

'You'd better come in,' said Fergus. 'Let's sit at the table and you can show me what you've brought.'

Sam spread out the folders on the table and Fergus picked one up. He began to read the first page, his eyes on stalks as he took in the contents. Sam looked around his office. Apart from the table and chairs, a large desk with a computer on it took up the far end of the room. There were some generic pictures of London at night adorning the walls and a sideboard with a decanter of what appeared to be whisky nestled among some heavy cut glass tumblers.

Fergus put down the folder and looked her in the eye.

'Where did you get this?' he said.

'I'm afraid I can't tell you,' she said.

'But it's dynamite. Edward Beckett has a high profile in the City. He's got some powerful friends too. What's in the other folders?'

'More of the same,' said Sam. 'We have copies of everything documented to the tiniest detail.'

'Holy crap. I think I need a drink.'

Fergus stood up and poured some whisky into a tumbler.

'Will you have one?' he said. 'I'm afraid I don't have a gin and tonic.'

'Yes, please,' said Sam.

While she sipped her whisky, Fergus reviewed the contents of the other two folders. He took out a notepad and made some notes, muttering and shaking his head. Finally, he put it down.

'This certainly qualifies as a scoop, if it's authentic,' he said.

'I can guarantee it,' said Sam.

'Oh, I don't doubt your word, but I need to do some fact-checking before I can get this published. What's your timetable on this?'

'As soon as possible would be perfect,' said Sam.

'I see your patience hasn't improved,' said Fergus, chuckling. 'You amaze me.'

He looked deep into her eyes and a blush rose up Sam's neck searing the roots of her hair.

'You know, of course, that your new career will evaporate when this gets out.'

'I thought it might,' said Sam.

'But what will you do?'

'I don't know. I suppose I'll have to search for a field contract abroad. London's not been a great success. People are only interested in the Sam Harris who got taken hostage, not the one who needs a job.'

'Your face lights up when you talk about your field work. I've never seen you animated when it comes to City life. Maybe you should consider it.'

'I'm not sure yet. I need some time to think,' said Sam.

'Start thinking about yourself for once. I'm not the only one who's getting older,' said Fergus.

'So, can you do it?'

'I can. Give me a few days to check it out. With Christmas around the corner, we are looking at publishing in the first week of January.'

Sam swallowed the rest of her whisky.

'You have my number,' she said.

After Sam had left, Fergus stared out of the window into the starless night. The yellow streetlights barely illuminated the wet streets filled with hunched shadows streaming home under black umbrellas. He should be on his way home by now, but he needed space to think and Aimee could be needy when he got home. She insisted on hearing all about his day, something he found hard to elaborate on, followed by a blow-by-blow description of her day to the minutest detail.

He tried to be interested, but what he really wanted sat in a bottle under the counter with a label covered in sloe berries. Aimee did not approve of his nightly gin and tonic habit, preferring to make him an infusion of chamomile or some other herbs tasting of silage 'for your nerves'. While he appreciated the wild sex that resulted when they got to bed, he found his attention had been wavering since he had found Sam again.

When he met Aimee, she seemed like the ideal companion, pretty, independent, with her own group of friends. But as time had gone on, she had become clingy and dependent and her friends had moved back to France or got married and changed social circles. She wanted to drag Fergus onto the married circuit and for a while he had gone with the flow.

But then Sam had turned up. She had, as usual, shaken him out of his comfort zone and made him feel things he tried to block out. He shouldn't have met her for coffee, but the temptation was too great. He reasoned that he had to tell her about Aimee, but really, he just wanted to watch her animated face as she sat across the table from him and told her self-deprecating stories of Derring-Do.

There didn't seem to be any danger in having a quick coffee but when her heart broke in front of him, a rush of genuine emotion flooded through his being scaring him with its intensity. He had forgotten how it felt to love someone like that and it frightened him back into Aimee's arms. There he stayed and smothered his feelings by directing them at her instead. Somehow, she diluted them in a flood of gush. But now he found himself in the office remembering Sam's thin body, racked with malaria, as he lifted her tenderly into the bath.

'I hate you, Sam Harris,' he said, with a total lack of conviction, surprising only the cleaning lady, who already avoided him because of his habit of speaking to himself. Embarrassed, he picked up his keys and headed downstairs to the parking garage in the basement.

Chapter XXXVIII

'You already know what this is,' said Hannah, handing Sam a rectangular package.

Sam grinned and ripped off the paper. The share certificate from Sierramar Holdings nestled in a little gold frame, now valueless except for the memories it evoked.

'Thank you, sis,' said Sam. 'I love it.'

She reached into the almost empty present bag beside her and pulled out a red envelope with a gold border. She stood up and handed it to her father who took it and turned it over a few times.

'What is this?' he said.

'It's for you both, from me,' said Sam.

Bill Harris opened the envelope with his trusty penknife and removed a letter written on Barclay's paper. He held it in the air with a questioning look at Sam who could hardly contain herself.

'Read it out loud,' she said.

Bill put on his reading glasses and took a deep breath.

'Dear Mr Harris. We are writing to inform you that your business loan has been reinstated from the date of this letter. The bank would like to apologise to you for any distress caused by what amounts to a severe clerical error. We shall cover the December and January interest payments as a gesture of goodwill. Happy Christmas. Best wishes B. Harrington, manager.'

Bill adjusted his glasses on his nose and raised one of his new handkerchiefs to dab his eye as he passed the letter to his wife. She let out an involuntary exclamation as she reread the letter.

Hannah took the letter next, reading it as if Sam had not read it out. Matilda Harris sniffed loudly and borrowed her husband's handkerchief.

'Oh my God, Sam. How did you do this? How...'

She tailed off and burst into tears, slipping off the sofa and crawling over to her parents, where she hugged her mother's legs.

'It's a miracle,' her father said. 'I feel like Tiny Tim.'

Sam smiled.

'That makes me Scrooge. I hate to ruin your Christmas but Mike Morton gets part of the credit. If it wasn't for him, Edward would have got away with this.'

'Mike Morton? There's a lot you haven't been telling us,' her father said. 'Fill the glasses, I think we'll be here a while.'

***

Edward Beckett raised a glass of champagne to his son. They had eaten in the restaurant of an exclusive London hotel and now they relaxed in a side room with a blazing fire.

'To Yubou,' said Edward.

Steven reciprocated with a sigh of contentment, rubbing his expanding stomach with relish.

'I wonder how Sam's Christmas is going,' said Edward.

'They're probably packing boxes as we speak,' said Steven 'It's the best present you could have given me.'

Edward chuckled.

'She had it coming. I've waited for years to get my revenge. It's just a pity I couldn't get Mike Morton too.'

'There'll be opportunities for that,' said Steven.

***

Fergus rubbed his eyes and faked a bleary smile. Aimee resembled one of Santa's elves on acid bounding around the house saying 'it's Christmas' repeatedly until Fergus thought he would explode with irritation.

'Come on, sleepyhead. Get up. I can't wait to see my presents.'

Her presents? A cold chill of panic gripped Fergus's chest. He had been working on the breaking story about Edward Beckett on Christmas Eve, chasing up a lead who had offered to confirm some of Edward's nefarious dealings in return for a few stiff whiskies. Somehow his intention of doing a proper Christmas shop for Aimee dissolved like the ice in their drinks.

When he emerged from the Fleet Street bar, his legs wobbled under him and he had difficulty focussing. He could imagine the row if he announced he had nothing to give her. Unthinkable. Instead, he staggered to the local garage shop and all-night chemist and cobbled together a selection of gifts which included a book about Boyzone, a bottle of Issey Miyake perfume, and a box of Milk Tray.

His wrapping skills had diminished with every drink, and he ended up with a sorry looking scramble of paper and tape which she eyed with suspicion as it sat alongside her crafted parcels. His head threatened to explode as Aimee sang carols in the kitchen, crashing pots and pans together like a three-year-old child.

She made him open his presents first. As he had expected, the exquisitely wrapped boxes contained tasteful, expensive presents, a bit like their giver. Aimee, who had accepted his cries of appreciation as her due, opened his gifts in complete silence with a grim expression on her face. She sat looking at them for a full minute before she shot him a piercing glare.

'This is a joke, no? You play with me?'

Fergus forced out a laugh.

'It's a joke. You don't really think these are your real presents, do you? Wait here.'

He climbed the stairs and took a shoebox down from the top shelf of his wardrobe. In it, he found the small ring box containing his grandmother's engagement ring. Regret swamped him as he returned downstairs, but no option remained if he wanted to avoid disaster. He got down on one knee and offered her the open box.

Chapter XXXIX

'It's finished,' said Fergus. 'Do you want to read it before I send it for publication?'

'Yes, please. Shall we come to your office?' said Sam.

'We? Oh, you mean with Mike? I rather hoped we'd have lunch together.'

'Without Mike? I don't think he'd like that. He's been instrumental in helping me get the information to bring Edward down,' said Sam.

'Okay, another time then. I'll meet you here at eleven tomorrow morning.'

'Perfect. I'll call him and give him the address.'

'Okay, until tomorrow then.'

Sam put down the receiver. She would have loved to have a cosy lunch with Fergus but somehow it didn't seem appropriate now that he was engaged. She had no loyalty to Aimee, but every time she met Fergus, feelings surfaced that she had no control over. There would be only one chance to take Edward down and losing focus at the last minute might jeopardise their plans.

Mike could hardly contain himself when she told him.

'Can't we meet him today?' he said.

'It's ten o'clock,' said Sam. 'Rather late for an office visit.'

'Okay, but don't be late.'

Sam found Mike waiting outside Fergus's office building. Blue with cold, he stomped his feet and exhaled in short sharp breaths as Sam approached.

'I'm not late, am I?' said Sam, checking her watch. 'You should have waited inside.'

'No, I arrived early. You know what the tubes are like.'

Sam smiled. Mike could afford a taxi now, but old habits die hard. She took his arm.

'Come on. Let's find out what Fergus has got for us.'

Fergus shook Mike's hand and gave Sam a peck on the cheek.

'Come on in. You're both freezing. I'll turn up the thermostat.'

Sam made a pot of tea and they settled around the board table. The atmosphere was thick with intrigue.

'I've printed off some copies,' said Fergus. 'Why don't you read it first and then we can discuss the contents.'

Silence reigned while Sam and Mike read their way through the document. Mike whistled and slapped his thigh, chuckling to himself. Fergus watched Sam like a hawk taking in her total concentration and the way the hair fell across her face. Finally, both Sam and Mike had finished, and they sat contemplating the enormity of what Fergus had put together.

'Congratulations,' said Mike. 'He's dead and buried. Even Edward can't talk his way out of this one.'

'What do you think, Sam?' said Fergus.

'It's damning,' said Sam. 'I didn't realise you could write like this.'

'There are a lot of things you don't know about me,' said Fergus.

'The shit will hit the fan,' said Mike. 'We should stand well back.'

'You need not worry,' said Fergus. 'As a journalist, I protect my sources. Anyway, Edward will be too busy with the police to bother either of you.'

'Cheers,' said Sam, raising her teacup.

Chapter XXXX

Oblivious to the gathering storm, Edward moved Steven into his flat after New Year's Eve. Steven took a dim view of the sleeping arrangements.

'You can't seriously expect me to sleep on that,' he said, pointing at the sofa.

'Honestly, I don't know what you're whinging about,' said Edward. 'This is the first of a long line of deals, and I need to you to lock the investors into the Yubou project to get us back on track.'

'But it stinks of smoke,' said Steven.

'Smell the money,' said Edward. 'That's all that counts. Get calling.'

Steven harrumphed but set himself up at the kitchen counter and started to call in the funds. Despite several of the clients complaining about the timing, straight after Christmas when their funds had suffered in the end-of-year droop in the market, they all agreed to pay up.

Edward made regular forays to Barclays to check the balance of the account.

'There's still two clients who haven't deposited their share of the money,' said Edward. 'Can you put a rocket up them? Time is running out. I don't trust Leo to keep his mouth shut.'

Steven made the calls and received assurances that the cash would be in the account the next day. The men celebrated with an expensive dinner in Chelsea and stumbled to bed long after midnight. Edward took the telephone off the hook so they could sleep in.

The next morning, Edward sent a bleary Steven out for the newspapers.

'Don't forget the Financial Times. I want to check my shares.'

While Steven staggered to the newspaper shop, Edward made some coffee and tidied away Steven's bedding, tutting at the mess. He set the table for breakfast and made some toast. He contemplated putting a couple of eggs on to boil, looking at his watch. *What was keeping the boy?*

The door to the flat opened and Steven stood there, his face ashen.

'What took you so long?' said Edward. 'Have you been vomiting again?'

Steven handed him the papers without answering. Irritated, Edward grabbed the Financial Times and spread it out on the counter. He had to read the headline twice before it registered. *City Financier suspected of multiple investment scams.* The second line of the article named him. Edward sank onto one of the chairs.

'Oh my God,' he said. 'Where did they get this? Who? How…'

He stopped talking. Steven's appalled expression loomed across the table. Edward stood up again and paced the room. Without thinking, he put the receiver back on the hook. Almost immediately the telephone started to ring. When he did not answer it, Steven stretched out to pick it up.

'Don't touch it,' said Edward.

'But, Dad.'

'You idiot. Don't you understand what just happened? We have to get to the bank right now.'

'What are we going to do?' said Steven.

'We have to transfer the money before the funds are blocked.'

Edward dressed in the same clothes he had worn the night before and threw on his coat without shaving or washing his teeth. Steven sat at the table, speechless with shock.

'What are you sitting there for, you big lump? Come on.'

'You want me to come to the bank?'

'No, you must go home now. Don't answer the telephone. Don't speak to anyone.'

'But Dad—'

Edward grabbed him by the collar of his coat and shook him.

'Listen to me. You're not involved in any of this. I don't want you ruining your life. Go home and if anybody asks, I'm an absentee father who has abandoned you.'

Steven nodded, the enormity of the situation sinking in. Edward shoving him out of the apartment and onto the street.

'Go on. Get out of here. I'll contact you when I can.'

Steven snivelled.

'It was that bloody woman, wasn't it?' he said.

Edward froze.

'Yes, but not the one you're thinking of. Leave well alone and don't get involved. If I manage to salvage any funds, I'll see you right.'

Edward watched Steven's plump back disappear down the street and then got into a taxi. The bank sat on the corner only three blocks away but there was no time to lose. Edward jumped out of the taxi and tried to enter the building at a normal pace. He sat on a chair outside the manager's office pretending to write notes in his diary. His legs trembled and sweat soaked his dirty shirt under his heavy winter coat.

Fifteen minutes passed, some of the longest minutes of Edwards life. The client who had been talking to the bank manager was shown out and the manager's secretary came over to Edward.

'Nice to see you, Mister Beckett. Can you give the manager a minute? He's just on the phone.'

After an eternity, the secretary reappeared.

'Can you go in please, sir? He's ready for you now.'

Edward straightened his suit and took a couple of deep breaths. Then he breezed into the manager's office as if nothing had happened. The manager shook his hand and directed him to sit down.

'How can I help you today?' he said.

'I'd like to arrange a transfer,' said Edward. 'By the way, what's the total balance of the account.'

The manager looked at a printout.

'Eighteen million, eight hundred thousand pounds,' he said, without batting an eyelid. 'Do you want to transfer all of it?'

'Leave a balance of eight hundred thousand, please,' said Edward, a little deflated by the manager's response to his wealth. 'I'd like that transferred to my account in the Caymans.'

'Okay, can you wait here while I get the paperwork for you? It shouldn't take long.'

The manager left shutting the door behind him. Edward swallowed hard, trying to stay calm. He was so close. He stood up and walked to the window. Outside a group of blackbirds dug in the muddy grass for worms and some stray leaves blew across the sparse lawn.

Behind him, the door opened. Edward spun around, a big smile on his face. Two burly men entered. They did not return his smile.

'Edward Beckett?' said one of them. 'I'm Detective Sergeant Billings and this is DC Potter. Would you like to come with us, sir?'

Chapter XXXXI

A north wind added a nip to the air as Sam crossed the bridge over the Thames at Cannon Street and made her way to the Anchor. She pulled her coat shut and zipped it up, winding her scarf around her neck and stuffing it into the neckline. Footsteps behind her made her turn to check if Mike was arriving at the same time, but she couldn't spot anyone in the dark street. Shrugging, she pushed open the door and chose a corner table near the bar for their celebration.

Edward's fall from grace had been swift after the article came out. The tabloid press had had a field day with the lurid details of his illegal dealings. Ophelia featured in most of their coverage, confirming her role in the demise of his empire. Photographs of her wearing glamorous outfits decked the pages and there were rumours someone had asked her to write a book about her experiences with Britain's most notorious swindler.

When Sam called her to ask if she wanted to go for a coffee, Ophelia had laughed and said she didn't have a free morning for months ahead. Her friends had rallied round after the publication, thrilled to have a new scandal to fill their days. Ophelia did not seem to mind their fickle behaviour, she revelled in once more being the centre of attention. It was a little galling to be second best after all they went through together, but Sam understood.

Sam bought herself a gin and tonic and sipped it. Mike always arrived late for everything so she settled herself in to wait. She finished her drink after half an hour but Mike still didn't show up. He did not answer his cell phone, unusual even for him. After nearly an hour passed, she decided he must have experienced an emergency, and leaving a message with the barman in case Mike turned up, she put her coat and scarf back on and left the bar.

A man waited for her at the street lamp outside the pub. It took her a couple of seconds to recognise Steven. He had lost weight and there were black bags under his eyes. Sam looked around to see if the street contained anyone else, but it appeared empty. Steven walked up to her, clenching his fists by his sides. She waited, uncertain whether to run or face him.

'What are you doing here?' she said.

'I followed you. I've been waiting for you to come out,' he said.

'What do you want?' she said.

'Revenge,' he said. 'You've ruined my life, and my father's.'

Sam snorted.

'You did that all by yourselves. I didn't force you to operate share scams.'

'You shouldn't have interfered. You deserved all you got.'

'Interfered?' said Sam. 'Because of you and your father, I lost my job and my father almost lost his house. Your father stole the money I earned in Sierramar Holdings. Did he tell you that?'

'What money?'

'The money Mike Morton made using my shares in his pet food company.'

'You're lying.'

Steven spat out his gum and wrapped it in the blue paper he ripped off a new piece. He threw it on the ground. Sam waited for him to make a move but he wavered, uncertain.

'You shouldn't litter,' said Sam, and bent down to pick up the paper.

Steven lunged forward and kicked her leg from under her. Sam fell sideways and hit her head on the lamp post still holding the paper in her fist. She lay on the ground without moving.

'Sam?' said Steven. 'Stop messing around.'

But Sam did not answer.

Chapter XXXXII

It should have been so romantic, a new year's trip to Hatton Garden with Aimee to buy an engagement ring. He wanted her to have his grandmother's ring but instead of squeaking with excitement, she pouted and told him she had set her heart on a new ring to signify their new love. Her refusal of the ring surprised him, but at least she had been truthful about it. Maybe their age difference meant he had old-fashioned ideas about jewellery.

He had agreed to go shopping for a ring, and they stepped out of the taxi into the street that made up the diamond district of London. The buildings were an odd mix of nineteen-seventies blocks sandwiched between Regency buildings with jewellers' shops under awnings. They were not the only couple on the prowl that afternoon, but he didn't see many women with men who looked as if they were their fathers. It made him uncomfortable.

He trailed after Aimee as she window-shopped for about half an hour before choosing one of the most expensive. Fergus patted his wallet in an unconscious gesture as they entered the store to be greeted by an obsequious assistant who grazed them with a sarcastic once over before plastering a smile of welcome over his face.

'How can I help you today?' he asked.

'We'd like to see your engagement rings, please,' said Aimee.

The assistant pulled out a tray and explained the merits of the ones Aimee pointed out.

'Half a carat? We can do better than that, can't we?' she said to Fergus. 'I want a big rock so I can show off to my friends. The assistant smirked at Fergus who rolled his eyes in droll answer. He replaced the tray and moved along the cabinet to remove another tray with flashier rings. The only rocks Fergus could imagine were the ones forming in his heart.

He blamed himself for not picking up on her mercenary nature. She gave plenty of clues, but he had been so besotted with her French flair and elegance that he missed them all. They were unsuited in almost every way. He wondered if Aimee noticed too.

And then there was Sam. She would have been happy with a Hula Hoop. She had invaded his thoughts to the extent that he called Aimee 'darling', so afraid was he that he might call her Sam instead. He had made a terrible mistake, and he needed to right it before it was too late. He tugged Aimee's arm.

'Can we do this later?' he said. 'I'm getting a migraine.'

Aimee sulked all the way home, which made it easier for him to prepare his withdrawal speech. She would have a bout of hysteria but she would get over it. Now he had decided he couldn't wait to tell her so she would move out. She squeezed his arm, but he stared out of the window of the taxi counting the minutes until they got home.

Aimee attacked him when he told her and threatened to sue him. As he placed an ice pack on his bruised face, he breathed a sigh of relief at his narrow escape. Aimee had never showed him this side of her before. Thank goodness he found out before it was too late. He poured himself a whisky and watched the news.

The next morning, he realised he didn't know where to find Sam. The only thing he knew for sure was that she worked for Leo Giustra in Edward Beckett's clandestine office in Mayfair. It should be a good place to start. He switched on the answer phone in his office and headed for Dover Street, wrapping himself in a black wool coat against the freezing January wind.

The young woman at the reception desk treated him like a bad smell when she realised who he was.

'Leo is busy,' she said. 'I doubt very much he'll want to see you.'

'Just tell him I'm the journalist who broke the story on Edward Beckett.'

Kelly's face lit up with a bright smile.

'It was you?' she said. 'Sam is a dark horse and no mistake.'

Fergus did not have time to ask her to explain that remark. Leo appeared and beckoned him into the boardroom.

'So, you're Fergus,' he said. 'I can't decide whether to hit you or hug you.'

'Your PA didn't think much of me,' said Fergus.

'Don't mind her. She's thick as thieves with Sam. After how you behaved, you're lucky she didn't punch you. She's Scottish.'

'I made a mistake. It seems I'm an idiot, but it took me this long to realise I love her.'

Leo looked surprised.

'You love her? But I thought she and Mike were together.'

'Sam and Mike. Are you sure?'

Leo shook his head.

'I may have got it wrong. So, what are you doing here?'

It was Fergus's turn to be surprised.

'I'm looking for her. It's the only place I could think of where someone might tell me of her whereabouts.'

'But Sam's in hospital. She got attacked by someone outside a pub and knocked out. We're waiting for news.'

'Oh my God. She's a magnet for trouble. She'll be the death of me.'

Leo laughed.

'She'll recover,' he said. 'No one keeps Sam down for long.'

Pale as snow, Fergus stood up.

'Which hospital?' he said.

***

'Will she be all right?' said Hannah, white with shock after seeing Sam prostrate in the hospital bed, a drip attached to her arm.

'The doctors say there's nothing wrong with her. She will wake up when she is ready,' said Bill Harris.

'Bloody typical. She's doing this on purpose.'

'Sweetheart,' said Matilda Harris. 'That's not fair. Sam's—'

The door to the ward swung open with such force that it bounced off the rubber stopper beside the wall and hit the man coming in.

'Jaysus, even the doors have it in for me,' said the man.

Hannah stared at him, her eyebrows knitted together. He gazed at her transfixed and shook his head as if confused.

'You're not Sam, but you look just like her. Where is she?'

'I'm sorry,' said Matilda Harris. 'But who are you?'

'Fergus,' he said, as if that sufficed and looked around as if he wanted to flee.

'You're that Fergus?' said Hannah. 'You've got a cheek. What makes you think you're welcome here?'

'Don't be rude,' her father said. 'There's no need for that.'

'No need? He smashed her heart into smithereens, twice.'

Hannah put her hands on her hips and blocked his way. Fergus swayed, uncertain how to deal with the unexpected obstacle.

'Please, I must see her,' he said. 'There are things I need to say.'

'You must wait. She hasn't woken up yet,' her father said.

'I don't care. I'll say them anyway.'

He fixed Matilda Harris with a pleading look. She fiddled with the clasp of her handbag.

'Go on, but don't be long,' she said.

Fergus pushed past Hannah, who had not moved, to get to the door of Sam's room. He opened it, slipping in and closing it behind him. Hannah tried to follow him but Matilda put a hand on her arm.

'No, darling. This isn't the time.'

Inside the room, painted in hospital green and reeking of Dettol, Fergus approached the bed from the side without the drip. Sam lay quiet with her eyes shut and a strand of bleached hair across her cheek. A bruise which had not yet turned purple marked her jaw. Fergus removed the hair from her cheek.

He pulled a metal chair up to the bed, wincing as one of the feet screeched across the floor. Sam's breathing did not vary. He sat as close as he could and took her free hand. Finding it cold, he kissed it and breathed on it to heat it up. He leaned closer to her and lifted the hair from her ear.

'Sam,' he whispered. 'Don't hide in there. It's me, Fergus. I can imagine you're annoyed that I can only talk to you when you are unconscious but bear with me. I made a massive mistake. Again.'

Fergus stroked Sam's hair, searching for the right words.

'You're right. You are the one. I don't know if you still think I am. I wouldn't blame you if you don't want me. My timing's atrocious. But I love you and I won't change my mind. Please, Sam, don't leave me ever again.'

He brushed tears off his cheeks as his emotions got the better of him, almost missing a choking sound emanating from Sam's throat.

'What? What is it? Tell me,' he said.

'Shorts,' she croaked.

'You old faker,' said Fergus. 'You only did this to get my attention.'

Sam opened her eyes and winked.

'You're so full of shit,' she said. 'Bugger off and let me get some sleep.'

When Sam woke again, her parents were sitting beside her bed.

'Hello, darling,' her father said. 'Welcome back.'

Sam tried to sit up and almost fell out of bed. Her head pounded and swam as she fought for balance. Her mother grabbed her and settled her against the pillows.

'Don't walk before you can run,' she said.

'What happened?' said Sam. 'I went to meet Mike at the Anchor and he didn't turn up. Steven was there. I...'

She trailed off. Her mother took her hand, a strange expression on her face.

'I'm afraid he's dead, sweetheart.'

'Steven, but how?' said Sam.

'She means Mike,' her father said. 'I'm terribly sorry, Sam.'

'Dead? I don't believe it,' said Sam.

'He suffered a massive heart attack at his home,' her mother said. 'His wife found him sitting in his favourite chair all ready to go to the pub.'

Tears rolled down Sam's cheeks.

'I can't believe it,' she said. 'He finally began to live the life he always wanted and now he's dead.'

Chapter XXXXII

Mike's death knocked Sam for six. Once she had recovered enough, the hospital discharged her, and she went home to her parent's house where she spent a couple of days moping and looking at her photograph albums of the time she spent with Mike, Gloria and Alfredo in Sierramar.

The police had investigated the attack on Sam, but she pretended she didn't know her assailant. She suspected Steven called the ambulance and she couldn't find any reason to make him feel worse. The investigation into the assault delayed Mike's funeral, as the officer leading the investigation wanted to check for foul play, in case they could link his death to the attack on Sam. The autopsy results were due in a day or two but nothing would convince Sam that Mike's death could be because of anything other than his famous dicky heart.

Mike's wife rang to invite Sam to his funeral and she could not refuse. Perhaps Ophelia would turn up too after they had been Musketeers together in the downfall of Edward. Sam had developed a fondness for Ophelia despite her grand ways and petty tantrums.

Unable to stand mooning about in the house, Sam returned to the office to check her emails and redouble her efforts to save Leo's business. Kelly met her at the top of the stairs and gave her a big hug.

'Nice to have you back. Are you sure you're ready?' said Kelly.

'As ready as I'll ever be. Shaken, but that's expected.'

'I'm sorry about Mike. That was a terrible shock.'

'I'm still taking it in. He had been looking ill for some time but I had no idea how bad it had become. I had become attached to him after working together again, even though he had his faults.'

The sound of giggling reached them from Leo's office.

'What on earth's going on in there?' said Sam.

Kelly winked.

'See for yourself,' she said.

Sam knocked on the door.

'Come in,' said Leo. 'It's open.'

Kelly raised her eyebrows at Sam who pushed open the door. Leo sat at his desk with a large whisky and sitting opposite him, Ophelia Beckett who smirked at Sam's astonishment.

'I see you two have met,' said Sam.

'You could say that,' said Ophelia.

'Meet the new boss,' said Leo

Ophelia threw her head back and giggled like a girl. Her Botox had worn off and enough muscles in her face worked to show how beautiful she was before she started attacking the symptoms of old age.

'Don't be silly, Leo,' she said, patting his hand.

He beamed back at her. Surely, they couldn't be an item?

'Does this mean Resource Ventures will live on?'

'Only if we can come up with a deal. You are staying, aren't you?'

'For now, anyway,' said Sam. 'I need time to sort out my head if that's all right with you.'

'You take your own sweet time,' said Ophelia. 'I'll keep the office afloat for as long as I'm able, which should be about fifty years with the money I'll get from Edward's hidden millions.'

She laughed.

'I've been fielding calls from Edward's investors. The bank put a stop on Edward's account before he transferred the money for Yubou to Henri Kanté. These clients are so impressed by your work on this that they want to use Resource Ventures to find them something else,' said Leo.

'That's great news,' said Sam. 'You must be thrilled.'

'It means we need to get working on a new project as soon as possible. Are you okay to start now?' said Leo. 'Or will you come in next week?'

'Yes, raring to go. I'd like to get started today if that's all right with you,' said Sam.

'Good. A package arrived for you from South America, Sierramar, I think. Maybe it's a project for us?'

The package lay on her desk amongst several other pieces of mail. Mystified, Sam picked it up and opened the plastic DHL wrapper. She tipped out a file and a handwritten note which she read with difficulty because of the squiggly writing. She beamed and sifted through the contents of the file, sitting down at her desk and almost missing her chair such was her concentration.

Kelly brought her a cup of tea.

'Any good?' she said.

'Better than good,' said Sam. 'It's a project I know well. The owner is a friend of mine. His funding has fallen through and he needs five million dollars for his next exploration season. I've visited the area several times and already visited their core shed so the due diligence has been done.'

'Why has he sent it to you?'

'He wants us to find the funding for him.'

'Leo will be ecstatic,' said Kelly.

'Let me finish reading first. I'll write him a summary page and then we'll see what he says.'

Sam had just finished the synopsis of the project when her cell phone rang. The display showed Fergus's name.

'Hello, stranger,' said Fergus. 'I thought you might like a spot of lunch with me to celebrate your triumphant return to the land of the living.'

'I'd like that,' said Sam.

'Can you manage one o'clock at Le Caprice? I've got a reservation.'

Sam did not ask him why he already had a table reserved. No need to look a gift horse in the mouth.

'See you there,' she said.

Kelly raised an eyebrow when Sam announced she had a lunch date with Fergus.

'Is that wise?' she said.

'I have no idea, but we need to talk sometime. It might as well be today.'

Fergus rose to greet Sam as the waiter showed her to the table. He gave her a chaste peck on the cheek and she hid behind the menu, gathering herself for the conversation to follow.

'You look tired, Sam. Are you sure you should be back at work already?' said Fergus, pulling the menu away from her face.

'Mike's death has been hard to process on top of everything else, so I haven't been sleeping well,' said Sam. 'But I feel fine and I couldn't stay at home any longer.'

'I'm sorry about Mike. Leo told me you had a thing with him.'

Sam guffawed.

'I did not have a fling with Mike. He's married for a start. Leo added two and two together and made eleven as usual. Mike and I worked together years ago, that's all.'

Fergus breathed a sigh of relief.

'I guess that makes more sense. Mike's not exactly your type.'

'Oh, and what is my type?' said Sam, trying not to laugh.

'I hoped it might be me,' said Fergus, avoiding her inquiring glance.

'You? But what about your fiancé?' said Sam, blushing traffic light red.

'I broke up with her.'

'What happened?' said Sam.

'I realised I was marrying the wrong woman.'

'I'm sorry.'

'Are you? I thought you'd be thrilled considering…'

Fergus looked deep into her eyes and she felt dizzy.

'Considering what?' she said.

'Well, you said you'd been waiting for me and—'

The waiter appeared at the table. He did not appear to notice the awkward silence.

'What will madam have?' he said, pen poised.

They ordered their food, and he scurried away again.

'You were saying?' said Sam, unwilling to let the matter drop.

'I thought you would give us another chance. I should have known it was you all along.'

Sam fiddled with her napkin. She had half expected Fergus to proposition her but the scenario included a bottle of wine and a lazy lunch with flirting first. His honesty caught her off guard. He reached across and took her hand.

'I don't expect you to tell me right away,' said Fergus. 'I just wanted to plant the seed. Aimee was a mistake. I should never have proposed to her. I guess the idea of a lonely middle age got to me.'

Sam removed her hand as gently as possible. She should have been thrilled, but the offer confused her.

'I can't discuss this now. I need time to think and get over the last few weeks before my mind clears. Let's have a delicious lunch and talk about Edward and Mike and journalistic scoops instead. Is that okay?' she said.

A shadow crossed over Fergus's face, but he smiled.

'We have plenty of time,' he said.

Chapter XXXXIII

Sam hated funerals but a need for closure drove her to the frigid cemetery in the East End where, to her surprise, hundreds of people spread across the bleak slope, hugging their coats tight against the wind. Clouds of steam from their breath made it seem as if mist had fallen on the funeral like an ethereal cloak.

Mike's death had overwhelmed her with sadness. She took a deep breath and forced the tears back. She had worked with Mike on her first contract in Sierramar and her life had never been the same since. His complete lack of responsibility had infuriated her, but time had cast its rosy hue over those memories, and she could only picture his cheery demeanour and protective attitude to Gloria, still her best friend. His cockney tones had echoed in her head from time to time over the years. Now she felt bereft, and not even the thought of Edward in a cell awaiting trial could ease the pain.

She shivered in the north wind which cut across the graveyard, whipping around the gravestones and making the poplars sway. Mike's widow stood with their two children: his son, taller than him but almost a carbon copy, the muscles working in his jaw and his daughter, a bottle-blond with mascara running down her cheeks. A horse-drawn carriage had transported the coffin, and the horses neighed and whinnied on the road behind the gravesite.

Sam scanned the rows of mourners facing her to distract herself from crying. She spotted Ophelia Beckett standing apart from the crowd, looking at the ground as if embarrassed. The cold emphasised her tight face and bloated lips, making her look like someone who had tried to escape old age and ended up resembling a species of fish with straggly, blonde hair. She wore a necklace of gemstones on her exposed bony chest. Sam couldn't stop staring at her in horrified fascination.

Then Ophelia raised her head and spotted Sam across the grave. She made a friendly gesture, beckoning Sam to her side. Sam made her way around the grave apologising as she parted the black sea of mourners.

'He always was a caution, even as a little boy,' said one old woman to her. 'He slipped in and out of our house all the time, escaping the wrath of his mother.'

She sniffed. Sam choked back a sob and forced herself to keep going. She would have loved to hear about Mike's childhood misdemeanours. Perhaps at the wake.

When she got to where Ophelia was standing, a bony hand in a lace glove grasped hers and did not release it. She felt oddly comforted. They stood in the pale sunlight until the vicar sent Mike on his way and the crowd sealed his voyage with a loud amen. One by one, people came forward and dropped crumbs of earth on the coffin.

Some young women dressed in tiny black leather miniskirts and bomber jackets flung roses into the dirt.

'Goodbye, darling,' said one. Sam realised it was the girl from the disco. Mike's wife didn't blink when they hugged her and offered condolences. Some men from the funeral followed them out of the cemetery to the nearest pub.

Sam followed the mourners back to Mike's house, an impressive three-storey Georgian terraced house. The neatly pointed bricks and shiny green door spoke of recent renovation and loving care. The ground floor heaved with people telling stories about Mike's escapades over the years. The solemn air at the funeral had been replaced by barking laughs and communal giggling as his sordid attempts to get rich were aired between victims and admirers. No ill will permeated the rooms despite this.

Seeking refuge, Sam parked herself on a sofa in the corner where Ophelia perched listening to the gossip and remembrance.

'This is a lovely house. I don't know what I was expecting—'

Ophelia cut her off.

'He bought it after he made a fortune in the dot-com boom. Edward was spitting.'

'Oh, I didn't realise.'

A warm glow enveloped Sam as she enjoyed this tale. Mike had made it big. How ironic that he did not live long enough to enjoy it. Before she could reply, a tap on her shoulder made her jump.

'I'm sorry, I didn't mean to startle you.'

Mike's widow, Emily, had come over and was hovering beside them.

'Sit down for God's sake,' said Ophelia.

'Not now. I wanted a word with Sam.'

'With me?'

'If that's okay.'

'Of course.'

Sam stood suddenly, sloshing her cup of tea into her saucer, dripping onto the Persian rug covering the floor.

'Don't worry about that,' said Emily. 'It's seen a lot worse from the dogs.'

She led Sam up the stairs, squeezing past a no-entry notice board that blocked the way and entering a small sitting room at the top of the stairs. The book-lined room had a sewing machine in the corner with a patchwork quilt still pinned under its foot. Emily reached up to grab something from the top shelf. She placed it in Sam's hand.

'He would have wanted you to have this,' she said.

The golden llama sat in the palm of Sam's hand, as beautiful as the day she had received it from Don Moises in the Sierramar jungle. She gasped.

'But I thought he gave it to Edward,' she said.

'Oh, I told him not to bother. Edward always treated Mike like shit. He didn't deserve it. Have you got your money yet?'

'My money?'

Sam's bewildered expression made Emily laugh.

'Your money from the will. You know.'

'I'm sorry. I don't know what you mean.'

A funny expression crossed Emily's face.

'Oh,' she said. 'I've remembered now. He was on his way to tell you when he...'

'I'm so sorry,' said Sam. 'Maybe he'd still be alive now if—'

'Don't say that. It's not true. Mike was a walking heart attack. The doctors told him to lose weight, but he just didn't care. He's the only one to blame.'

She sobbed and blew her nose before blowing her cheeks out. She wrung the handkerchief between her plump fingers and looked up at Sam's concerned face.

'Anyway, he's gone now. And you need that money.'

'I still don't understand.'

'Mike felt so bad about Edward stealing your money that he wrote you into his will. He knew he hadn't long to live, and he wanted to do something for you. He asked my permission a few weeks ago, and I agreed. I thought I'd asked you to the reading of the will, but it slipped my mind with the autopsy and the funeral and all that. He wanted you to be financially independent. He really cared about you.'

Sam's eyes filled with tears and mouth fell open in astonishment. Her mind raced, and she blurted out the first thing that came to it.

'How much money?'

'Nearly five hundred thousand pounds.'

Sam blanched and took a deep breath.

'What?' she said.

'Half a million pounds. Are you all right?'

'Um, no, I can't believe it.'

Her head was swimming. Half a million pounds? She stood up abruptly, and regretted it, almost fainting on her feet.

'I've got to go,' she said.

'Oh, I hope I haven't upset you. It must be a bit of a shock.'

Sam forced a smile.

'A good shock. Thank you so much for telling me. I loved Mike too. You must miss him terribly.'

'We had some good times together despite everything. I would have liked to have more time, but it wasn't to be.'

'Do you mind if I go for a walk now? I need to digest this news and get some air. Will you come with me?'

'That's okay, love. I've got to stay and entertain the mourners and make sure no one urinates in the Chinese vases. Drop in for a cup of tea soon and tell me about your adventures with Mike in Sierramar. I've always wondered what really happened.'

That made Sam bite her lip and produce a real smile. What on earth had he told her? Or Edward for that matter. The truth seemed unlikely.

'The lawyer is holding the money for you. Why don't you call him and organise a transfer?' said Emily. 'Wait a minute. I have his card here.'

She fumbled in a drawer and pulled it out, handing it to Sam with a smile.

'I will. Thank you. And I promise to come soon and tell you some tall tales.'

Emily hugged her and they both struggled not to weep. Sam stumbled downstairs, grabbing her coat, and opened the heavy hall door. Once outside she strode to the underground station, the wind cutting through her coat but unable to cool the excitement bubbling up through her body.

She was rich, well not exactly rich, but rich enough. Mike had always been economical with the truth, but this seemed real enough. She would keep her windfall a secret until it was in her account. Her family had suffered enough disappointments in the last few months.

Hot air blew up the underground stairs welcoming her into its warm embrace. She showed her return ticket to the man at the barrier and rode the escalator into the bowels of the earth. Not even the flasher at Oxford Circus could affect her elation. She waved at him and smiled as he stood legs akimbo on the platform with his coat wide open as they drew out. This so confused him he dropped one side of his coat to give her a half-wave back.

Chapter XXXXIV

Matilda Harris went quiet, and then burst into tears, when Sam told her parents about the money.

'Don't cry, mummy, this is good news,' said Sam. 'I can buy myself a house.'

'It's just such a shock,' her mother said.

'Mike Morton. Who'd have imagined it?' said Bill. 'I can scarcely believe he came good after all these years.'

'People change,' said Sam. 'Mike was aware he only had a short time left and his wife told me he wanted to make it right with me.'

'But so much money,' her mother said. 'It's a miracle.'

'You deserve it, darling. Slow and steady, and honest, wins the race,' her father said.

Hannah screamed with delight when Sam asked her to go house hunting with her.

'I can't believe it. Of course, I'll come with you. There's a nice little house around the corner from me we can visit.'

The two sisters visited a dozen houses recommended by the estate agent but Sam settled on the first one they saw, a house in the street parallel to her sister's place. The house had been empty for a year so the sale went through within weeks. Hannah and Sam collected the keys together, and let themselves into Sam's new home.

A swell of emotion flooded through Sam as she stepped into the hall.

'Thanks, Mike,' she said, moved to tears.

'He came good in the end, the old reprobate,' said Hannah. 'Do you need help moving your stuff in?'

'I'm not organised yet. I'll let you know. It's going to be so nice having you around the corner,' said Sam.

'You can't bear to be parted from me,' said Hannah. 'We can be two old maids together.'

'Speak for yourself,' said Sam. 'I've got offers.'

Hannah's eyes widened.

'Well, you're a dark horse,' she said. 'First large inheritances, and now you've got offers. Tell me all about it.'

They sat in a local café and drank steaming cups of tea at a table in the window.

'Come on. Spill the beans,' said Hannah.

'It's Fergus,' said Sam.

'Fergus?' said Hannah. 'But isn't he engaged to that young French woman?'

'They broke up after Christmas. He told me he was marrying the wrong woman.'

Hannah frowned.

'That sounds a bit clichéd to me.'

'He can be corny. It's just, um, I'm not sure.'

'But you said he was the one?'

'He was, is, I'm not sure anymore.'

'Do you want my honest opinion?' said Hannah.

'Do I have any choice?'

Hannah sighed.

'I know it's none of my business. But if he is still the one, you should be sure. When Simon asked me to marry him, I didn't hesitate for a second.'

Sam raised an eyebrow.

'Yes, I'm aware I'm divorced, but at the time I just knew. You shouldn't have doubts. It's a bad sign. And anyway…'

She tailed off.

'Anyway, what?' said Sam.

'Are you sure you want to get married? It's not as if you've ever had the ambition to settle down. Being married is hard work. You can't march off to the jungle every time you feel like it, especially if you have children. What I mean is, are you sure you're ready?'

Sam sighed.

'No. I'm not. And the way he dumped Aimee like a hot potato and transferred his affections to me has unsettled me.'

'What do you mean?'

'Well, what if he does the same to me when something better comes along? Maybe when we're knee-deep in nappies, he won't feel so romantic.'

'I can't tell you what to do, but be careful, Sam. You're fragile right now with everything that happened. Don't grab the first thing that comes along just to get a little peace.'

After her conversation with Hannah, Sam rang the estate agent and asked them to let out her house for a year. Hannah was right. She needed some space to think before she took such a giant leap of faith. But then she rang the estate agent again and cancelled the order.

'Are you staying?' said Hannah. 'I thought you were going to give it some time?'

'No, I'm going,' said Sam. 'But I'll be away at least a year and I thought you might like to move in instead.'

'Me? But why?'

'Well, if you live here you can save your rent towards a deposit, and I can keep my stuff in the house without worrying about it. What do you think?'

Hannah's eyes opened wide.

'Really?'

'I thought the children could have the main bedroom and you could use the second bedroom. It's not a lot smaller.'

Hannah gave her a hug.

'How wonderful. I accept. Thank you, sis.'

Having dealt with the house, ringing Gloria's number in Sierramar was Sam's next task, an easy one.

'Hi, chica. Can I come and stay with you and Alfredo? I need a holiday.'

Gloria squealed.

'When are you coming? Can you bring me some tea? And chutney. And mint jelly.'

'Send me a list,' said Sam, laughing. 'I'll let you have my flight details as soon as I book it.'

Her parents showed no surprise when Sam said she was off to Sierramar.

'That sounds lovely, darling. You've had a tough time. Gloria will soon cheer you up,' her father said.

'One of these days, your father and I will have to come with you,' her mother said. 'I've always wanted an adventure.

Epilogue

A gentle breeze blew through the palm trees, ruffling the fronds and making the coconuts sway on their stalks. In front of her, the golden sand glittered in the afternoon sunlight and small waves crept up the beach making the tiny crabs scurry up the slope. Sam sighed in contentment as the sun caressed her skin.

A twig cracking behind her alerted her to the presence of Yannis, who had closed the restaurant after the lunch shift and come to join her on the beach. He came up close behind her, the heat from his body making her lean into his chest. He ruffled her sun-bleached hair with calloused fingers. Sam reached backwards from the table where she had placed the new laptop and pulled him down for a kiss.

'Have you started your book yet?' he said. 'I'm dying to read all about your adventures.'

'Not yet, but there's no shortage of material. How hard can it be?'

Thank you for reading my book. If you enjoyed it, won't you please take a moment to leave me a review at your favourite retailer?

Thank you

PJ Skinner

This is the last book in the series but more books are in the pipeline.

Check my Author page for details

All my books are available in paperback from your favourite retailer.

Other Books in the Sam Harris Adventure Series

Fool's Gold - Book 1

Newly qualified geologist Sam Harris is a woman in a man's world - overlooked, underpaid but resilient and passionate. Desperate for her first job, and nursing a broken heart, she accepts an offer from notorious entrepreneur Mike Morton, to search for gold deposits in the remote rainforests of Sierramar. With the help of nutty local heiress, Gloria Sanchez, she soon settles into life in Calderon, the capital. But when she accidentally uncovers a long-lost clue to a treasure buried deep within the jungle, her journey really begins.

Teaming up with geologist Wilson Ortega, historian Alfredo Vargas and the mysterious Don Moises, they venture through the jungle, where she lurches between excitement and insecurity. Yet there is a far graver threat looming; Mike and Gloria discover that one of the members of the expedition is plotting to seize the fortune for himself and is willing to do anything to get it. Can Sam survive and find the treasure or will her first adventure be her last?

The first book in the Sam Harris Series sets the scene for the career of an unwilling heroine, whose bravery and resourcefulness are needed to navigate a series of adventures set in remote sites in Africa and South America. Based on the real-life adventures of the author, the settings and characters are given an authenticity that will connect with readers who enjoy adventure fiction and mysteries set in remote settings with realistic scenarios.

Set in the late 1980's themes such as women working in formerly male domains, and what constitutes a normal existence, are examined and developed in the context of Sam's constant ability to find herself in the middle of an adventure or mystery. Sam's home life provides a contrast to her adventures and feeds her need to escape. Her attachment to an unsuitable boyfriend is the thread running through her romantic life, and her attempts to break free of it provide another side to her character.

Hitler's Finger - Book 2

The second book in the Sam Harris Series sees the return of our heroine Sam Harris to Sierramar to help her friend Gloria track down her boyfriend, the historian, Alfredo Vargas.

Geologist Sam Harris loves getting her hands dirty. So, when she learns that her friend Alfredo has gone missing in Sierramar, she gives her personal life some much needed space and hops on the next plane. But she never expected to be following the trail of a devious Nazi plot nearly 50 years after World War II …

Deep in a remote mountain settlement, Sam must uncover the village's dark history. If she fails to reach her friend in time, the Nazi survivors will ensure Alfredo's permanent silence. Can Sam blow the lid on the conspiracy before the Third Reich makes a devastating return?

The background to the book is the presence of Nazi war criminals in South America which was often ignored by locals who had fascist sympathies during World War II. Themes such as tacit acceptance of fascism, and local collaboration with fugitives from justice are examined and developed in the context of Sam's constant ability to find herself in the middle of an adventure or mystery. Sam's home life provides a contrast to her adventures and feeds

The Star of Simbako - Book 3

A fabled diamond, a jealous voodoo priestess, disturbing cultural practices. What could possibly go wrong? The third book in the Sam Harris Series sees Sam Harris on her first contract to West Africa to Simbako, a land of tribal kingdoms and voodoo.

Nursing a broken heart, Sam Harris goes to Simbako to work in the diamond fields of Fona. She is soon involved with a cast of characters who are starring in their own soap opera, a dangerous mix of superstition, cultural practices and ignorance (mostly her own). Add a love triangle and a jealous woman who wants her dead and Sam is in trouble again. Where is the Star of Simbako? Is Sam going to survive the chaos?

This book is based on visits made to the Paramount Chiefdoms of West Africa. Despite being nominally Christian communities, Voodoo practices are still part of daily life out there. This often leads to conflicts of interest. Combine this with the horrific ritual of FGM and it makes for a potent cocktail of conflicting loyalties. Sam is pulled into this life by her friend, Adanna, and soon finds herself involved in goings on that she doesn't understand.

The Pink Elephants - Book 4

Sam gets a call in the middle of the night that takes her to the Masaibu project in Lumbono, Africa. The project is collapsing under the weight of corruption and chicanery engendered by management, both in country and back on the main company board. Sam has to navigate murky waters to get it back on course, not helped by interference from people who want her to fail. When poachers invade the elephant sanctuary next door, her problems multiply. Can Sam protect the elephants and save the project or will she have to choose?

The fourth book in the Sam Harris Series presents Sam with her sternest test yet as she goes to Africa to fix a failing project. The day to day problems encountered by Sam in her work are typical of any project manager in the Congo which has been rent apart by warring factions, leaving the local population frightened and rootless. Elephants with pink tusks do exist, but not in the area where the project is based. They are being slaughtered by poachers in Gabon for the Chinese market and will soon be extinct, so I have put the guns in the hands of those responsible for the massacre of these defenceless animals

The Bonita Protocol - Book 5

An erratic boss. Suspicious results. Stock market shenanigans. Can Sam Harris expose the scam before they silence her? It's 1996. Geologist Sam Harris has been around the block, but she's prone to nostalgia, so she snatches the chance to work in Sierramar, her old stomping ground. But she never expected to be working for a company that is breaking all the rules.

When the analysis results from drill samples are suspiciously high, Sam makes a decision that puts her life in peril. Can she blow the lid on the conspiracy before they shut her up for good?

The Bonita Protocol is the fifth book in the Sam Harris Adventure series. If you like gutsy heroines, complex twists and turns, and heart pounding action, then you'll love PJ Skinner's thrilling novel.

Digging Deeper - Book 6

A feisty geologist working in the diamond fields of West Africa is kidnapped by rebels. Can she survive the ordeal or will this adventure be her last? It's 1998. Geologist Sam Harris is desperate for money so she takes a job in a tinpot mining company working in war-torn Tamazia. But she never expected to be kidnapped by blood thirsty rebels.

Working in Gemsite was never going to be easy with its culture of misogyny and corruption. Her boss, the notorious Adrian Black is engaged in a game of cat and mouse with the government over taxation. Just when Sam makes a breakthrough, the camp is overrun by rebels and Sam is taken captive.
Will anyone bother to rescue her, and will she still be alive if they do?

You can order these books in paperback at your favourite retailer.
Please go to the PJSKINNER.com website for links.

Connect with the Author

If you would like updates on the latest in the Sam Harris Series or to contact the author with your questions please click on the following links:
Website: www.pjskinner.com
Facebook:
https://www.facebook.com/PJSkinnerAuthor
Twitter: https://twitter.com/PJSkinnerAuthor
Amazon Author page

About the Author

PJ Skinner is the author of the Sam Harris Series of adventure-thriller novels. A geologist who has spent thirty years roaming the planet and collecting tall tales and real-life experiences, she now writes fact-based novels from the relative safety of London. She still travels worldwide collecting material for the series and having her own adventures.

The author is working on other new books, one of which, Rebel Green, is being written with the help of a childhood spent in Ireland.

The Sam Harris Adventure Series will appeal to lovers of adventure thrillers. It has a unique viewpoint provided by Sam, a female interloper in a male world, as she struggles with alien cultures and failed relationships.

www.ingramcontent.com/pod-product-compliance
Lightning Source LLC
Chambersburg PA
CBHW050829190726
48286CB00007B/2014